MASTER OF THE MOUNTAIN

Cherise Sinclair

Author's Note

To my readers,

This book is fiction, not reality and, as in most romantic fiction, the romance is compressed into a very, very short time period.

You, my darlings, live in the real world and I want you to take a little more time than the heroines you read about. Good Doms don't grow on trees and there's some strange people out there. So while you're looking for that special Dom, please, be careful.

When you find him, realize he can't read your mind. Yes, frightening as it might be, you're going to have to open up and talk to him. And you listen to him, in return. Share your hopes and fears, what you want from him, what scares you spitless. Okay, he may try to push your boundaries a little—he's a Dom, after all—but you have your safeword. You will have a safeword, am I clear? Use protection. Have a back-up person. Communicate.

Remember: safe, sane and consensual.

Know that I'm hoping you find that special, loving person who will understand your needs and hold you close. Let me know how you're doing. I worry, you know.

Meantime, come and hang out with the Masters.

~ Cherise

Praise for the writing of Cherise Sinclair

Master of the Mountain

"...a very sexy, sultry romance with depths and layers that make it fascinating."

– Kimberly Spinney, *Sensual Reads*

Club Shadowlands

"*Club Shadowlands* is a superbly crafted story that will dazzle any BDSM fan and have them adding it to their must read list!"

– Shannon, *The Romance Studio*

Dark Citadel

Dark Citadel is a decadent delight and an immensely satisfying read."

– Priscilla Alston, *Just Erotic Romance Reviews*

Breaking Free

"A riveting tale, *Breaking Free* is a book I highly recommend."

Jennifer Bishop, *Romance Reviews Today*

Lean on Me

"There is so much heat, sexual tension, and emotion that you can't help but long for more."

– Fern, *Whipped Cream Reviews*

LooseId®

ISBN 13: 978-1-60737-916-4
MASTER OF THE MOUNTAIN
Copyright © November 2010 by Cherise Sinclair
Originally released in e-book format in August 2009

Cover Art by Anne Cain
Cover Layout and Design by April Martinez

DISCLAIMER: Many of the acts described in our BDSM/fetish titles can be dangerous. Please do not try any new sexual practice, whether it be fire, rope, or whip play, without the guidance of an experienced practitioner. Neither Loose Id nor its authors will be responsible for any loss, harm, injury or death resulting from use of the information contained in any of its titles.

This book is an original publication of Loose Id. Each individual story herein was previously published in e-book format only by Loose Id and is a work of fiction. Any similarity to actual persons, events or existing locations is entirely coincidental.

Printed in the U.S.A. by
Lightning Source, Inc.
1246 Heil Quaker Blvd
La Vergne TN 37086
www.lightningsource.com

Chapter One

"You about there, babe?" Matt sounded as if he was gritting his teeth as he pumped into her. "You want me to rub you some more?"

Frustration congealed inside Rebecca like cold oatmeal. She was nowhere close to getting off, and every time he asked what to do, her orgasm receded further. No point in continuing. "Oooh," she sighed, jerking her hips up and down and clenching her vagina.

"Oh yeah." He groaned in relief, and again as he came a second later.

Well, hadn't that been exciting? *Not.* As Matt rolled over onto the mattress with a satisfied groan, Rebecca considered pushing him right out of the bed. But it wasn't his fault. He tried. He always tried, asking her if this technique worked or that one. How could she tell him that she wanted him to just know what to do?

She sure couldn't tell him she faked a good half her orgasms. And she resented that he couldn't tell, which was even more unfair. She didn't get off in an unmistakable fashion, after all. For her, an orgasm felt more like a sneeze, certainly not the earthquake her friends described, and nowhere close to the shrieks of pleasure from the apartment next door. What would that feel like? To be so overwhelmed as to actually scream?

Matt spoke up as if he'd followed her train of thought. "You know, Rebecca, you never seem all that enthusiastic about screwing. And my technique's fantastic."

So informed by all his previous girlfriends, undoubtedly. *Good to know. Thanks, Matt.* Now she felt really inadequate. Heck, they'd just cosigned a lease and moved in together a couple of weeks ago, and he was already bored with her. She swallowed past a tight throat. "Maybe we're not a good match." She rolled over and stared out her bedroom window, where the next-door apartment building glowed pink in the sunset.

"Oh, don't get like that." Matt patted her shoulder. "We're great together. Where would I find a woman who could be so polite during business dinners? And what other guy would let you drag him to an art show on Mission?"

"Well, that's true." She'd thought they were a perfect couple right from the beginning. Emulating her excruciatingly practical mother, Rebecca had created a list of the characteristics of her ideal man, and when she'd met Matt, she'd been stunned how well he matched her requirements. He was easygoing and charming. Well groomed with a sense of style. They enjoyed the same movies, books, and friends. They both had professional jobs, made about the same amount of money, and he was more metro than macho. He could actually converse about movie themes, and he liked Chinese food.

Maybe she should have included sex somewhere on the list, but she'd never considered it very important. Aside from sex, she and Matt were very compatible. She rolled back over with a sigh. "I guess you're right."

Lying on his back, Matt had a well-tended look with boutique shop-trimmed blond hair, muscles from dedicated gym usage, and a lingering tan from a business trip to San Diego. Tomorrow he'd get up, eat something low-fat and disgustingly healthy, and head off to his job at the brokerage house, content with life.

Her contentment matched his. *Really.* After all, the managing director of her ad agency was considering her for the position of senior art director, putting her on the fast track to the top. A gust of wind whipped the curtains inward, bringing the sea tang of San Francisco Bay and the scent of a spring rain. She lived in the best city in the world.

"I have an idea, but you probably won't like it." Matt turned to face her and propped himself up with an elbow. "I belong to this group, and we're taking a very long Memorial Day weekend in the mountains."

"I remember you said you'd be out of town." She bit her lip. Maybe they weren't as close as she'd thought. He'd never mentioned belonging to anything other than his fitness club and some business associations. "What group is this?"

"It's a swingers' club."

"Very funny." Only he wore no smile. He wasn't joking. "Seriously? Swingers, like in exchanging-partners swingers?"

He shrugged, half-embarrassed and half-smug. "That's it. We get together for a weekend every couple of months... Uh, seems like last time we met, you were in Chicago for a seminar. Anyway, there's about twenty in the club and—"

"You've been screwing around with twenty other people and are just now letting me know? God, Matthew, how many diseases have you given me?"

He held up his hand. "Don't lose it, babe. Everyone uses condoms and gets tested routinely. It's not like that."

The fist squeezing her insides relaxed slightly. "Well, that's good."

"And it's not like you and I have an exclusive relationship. Right?"

"True." Just because she didn't go out and screw the neighborhood didn't mean he couldn't. They'd both agreed to keep it loose. But good grief. Sure, her...libido...didn't match his, but who would have thought he'd take care of that little discrepancy in such a fashion?

And here she'd thought he was commitment-phobic because his last relationship had gone bad. She'd been forcing herself not to push him. *Duh, Rebecca.* "So you're going off to have an orgy?"

In the dim light from the living room down the hall, she saw him roll his eyes. "It's not an orgy. We swap, and sometimes two couples get together in a foursome, but not more than that. Usually." He grinned.

"Oh, well then, that's all right," she said drily.

"More can be really fun. Come with me this time, babe." He took her hand. "We take over this great place up in the mountains. There're rustic cabins scattered throughout the pines, and we're the only people there. We go up Friday, spend the weekend, Memorial Day, and Tuesday, then drive back on Wednesday. Nice people, amazing sex. You could even bring your paints."

"Rustic cabins?" She stared at him in disbelief. Vacations, not that she'd taken one since she left college, should be spent somewhere warm and sunny with room service. But she'd gotten off the subject. He was talking about sex. "Jumping in and out of bed with other people? Matt, I'm not into that."

The smile died from his face. "Rebecca, we need to add some spice to this relationship. It's…"

Inadequate. Lacking. The echo of the door slamming behind her father twenty-some years ago seemed to reverberate in her ears. "*You're fat and boring, and so's the kid. I'm leaving.*" Her ribs seemed to squeeze inward, compressing her lungs until she couldn't get a breath. She shook her head at him.

"Well," Matt added, "it's just not working out for me."

What he meant was *she* wasn't working out for him. How could she not have realized, have seen this coming? *What about my list and my plans?* "What about our lease?" she asked through numb lips.

"Oh, let's not get carried away here," he said lightly. "Just come with me this weekend. It'll be good for you. Maybe help you lose some of those inhibitions."

She bit back her first response—*no way*—because, as bluntly as he'd put it, he had a point. Their sex life lacked something… No, be honest, *she* lacked something. But messing around with a group? Going to bed with strangers? She just couldn't do something like that. "Matt…"

"Only for a weekend, babe. Give it a try."

A try. She tried to imagine it… *Probably some strange man would come into her room. And maybe she'd hesitate, so he'd grab her, pin her to the mattress, force her to cooperate*. Her clit started throbbing like she was sitting on her vibrator. "Well, maybe…"

He rubbed her shoulder. "I've really been wanting you to join us."

And if she didn't go, their relationship would end. That was all too clear. *No more boring*. "Amazing sex, huh? Why not?"

* * *

As the car bumped down the never-ending, rutted dirt road, Rebecca felt as if every bone in her body had turned to splinters. The car lights created a thin tunnel between the encroaching trees, then suddenly speared out across a wide clearing.

Serenity Lodge. Finally.

"At last." Matt echoed her thoughts as he pulled the car into a small parking area well concealed behind bushes and trees.

She sighed in relief that the drive was over. Then apprehension prickled across her nerves. "What happens now?"

Matt patted her leg. "Nothing's going on tonight. We'll just sign in, unpack, and make an early night of it."

"Good plan. I'm exhausted." The only swinging she wanted to do tonight was into a bed. Before leaving, she'd finished off the work on her desk, met with one account team, then with a copywriter. She couldn't afford to get behind, not with the manager watching her work.

She slid out of the BMW convertible and took a breath of air so cold and crisp, it burned her lungs. Looking up past the towering pines at the fat white dots in the black night, she blinked in surprise. Wow. Stars grew bigger outside of the city, didn't they? Had the sky looked like this before she and Mom moved to San Francisco after her parents divorced? "Can you believe these stars?"

"What, babe?" Matt called, head buried in the trunk.

"Nothing."

After pulling out the two suitcases, he slammed the trunk and handed over her bag.

They crossed the clearing to a massive two-story log building. Rebecca lugged her case across the wide, encircling porch and followed Matt into a huge room. Numerous leather couches, big armchairs in dark red upholstery, and brightly colored rag rugs created cozy sitting areas. On the left wall, a fire crackled in a stone fireplace bracketed by well-stuffed bookcases. Four men played cards at the far end.

A woman by the fire called a welcome to Matt, and suddenly people seemed to come out of the woodwork.

Matt beamed, shaking hands with the men and exchanging hugs with the women. "Rebecca, this is Paul and Amy."

Rebecca nodded and smiled, trying to put names to faces. Paul and Amy: a tall, balding man and a slender brunette with a dark tan. Ginger and Mel: a redhead and a beefy man. Serena and Greg: blonde woman, nerdy man with glasses.

Then she started losing track, but not enough to miss the fact that the men came in different sizes, but all the women were toned and slender. She sure didn't fit in if that was a criterion for acceptance. A sinking feeling pulled at her stomach; being the last person picked in gym class had sucked. Would these sexual calisthenics be the same?

"Nice to meet you all," she said, noting the bulky sweaters, T-shirts, and jeans. Very casual. Why hadn't Matt mentioned the dress code? She still wore her suit. Then again, she hadn't had much choice. Aside from two pairs of Ralph Lauren jeans, her entire wardrobe contained only business clothes, sweats, and more sweats covered with paint.

"Let's get signed in. Then we can haul our stuff over to the cabin," Matt said, pulling her toward a desk to the right of the front door.

A low growl halted her in her tracks. *A dog.* Her suitcase dropped to the floor as she recoiled. Heart thudding inside her chest, she fought to stand still and not run out the door. Any dog allowed inside couldn't be vicious. It couldn't.

"C'mon, Rebecca. Sign in." Matt gave her an impatient look.

"Right." She forced her feet forward, one hard-won step after another. Where was the dog? As the man behind the desk shook hands with Matt, Rebecca checked the floor. *There.* Standing beside the man, it looked huge, with dark brown fur and a darker muzzle. It stared at her, and she heard another rumble.

"Thor," the man said, his low voice almost a match for the dog's. "Down."

The dog flattened to the floor. It never stopped looking at her, though.

"Rebecca, this is Logan Hunt. He owns the place," Matt said.

"Hey, Matt!" one of the women yelled from the front door. "Come help us decide on tomorrow's plans."

"Be right there," he called back, then patted Rebecca's arm. "You go ahead and sign in. I'll be on the porch with Paul and Amy."

She nodded, unable to tear her gaze from the dog.

"Rebecca, eyes on me, not the dog." The deep, rough voice broke her free, and she turned to the owner. He looked as mean as his dog, with steel blue eyes in a deeply tanned face—a ruthless face decorated with a day-old beard and a white scar below his left cheekbone. After handing her a pen, he tapped the paper in front of him. "Name and address. Signature on the release."

"Release?"

His firm lips curved. "So you can't sue us if you fall down the mountain and break your neck."

Right. After filling out the paperwork, she picked up her suitcase, holding it in front of her just in case the dog moved. When the owner rose, she retreated a step. He stood at least an inch over six feet, with muscles straining his dark red flannel shirt. The rolled-up sleeves displayed thick forearms with heavy-boned, corded wrists. More scars graced his hands. Whatever he'd done in the past must have been brutal.

"I'll show you to your cabin." He walked over to her, and when the dog followed him, she couldn't seem to move. That animal would rend her to shreds, spilling her blood, tearing her...

"Open your hand, sugar." A flash of amusement showed in his eyes as he tugged the suitcase from her hand.

"Sorry," she whispered. Matt was already out the door; he'd left her, left her here with that dog.

It stared at her, growling.

"Thor, be nice," the man snapped.

The dog stopped, although Rebecca could see it wanted to bite her.

"He can tell you're scared, and he's going to play the bully." The man stepped closer until she had to look up at him—his dog wasn't the only bully in the place—but when his gaze met hers, somehow she knew he wouldn't let her be hurt.

Putting a hand on her lower back, he herded her toward the door.

Pretty little thing, Logan thought, with the biggest green eyes he'd seen in a long time. Ones that showed every emotion coursing through her—mostly fear, right now. What had brought a timid mouse into this herd of kinky yuppies?

He heard the click of the dog's toenails on the floor and turned. "Thor. Stay here."

After a long pause and a surely-you're-not-serious look, Thor walked slowly back to the desk and dropped down with a long-suffering sigh.

The oversize mutt could be a real drama queen. Logan grinned, then followed the mouse named Rebecca out the door.

Wasn't it interesting how her timidity disappeared the minute she realized Thor had stayed behind? Her posture straightened; her head came up. Now she actually looked like the professional woman the French-braided hair and deep blue suit proclaimed. Obviously a successful woman, for only that kind of expensive tailoring could manage to hide all a woman's best attributes. A shame, really. She had a lush body that screamed for highlighting, not hiding. And well made-up or not, she couldn't conceal the freckles dancing across her nose and cheeks.

As they waited for Matt to break loose of the two club members he'd joined, Logan leaned against a porch post. Damn, he was tired, right down to the bone. The two nightmares last night hadn't left him much sleep, especially the final one. He scrubbed his face with his hands. Bullets, rockets... Those weren't so bad. But the dreams of IED explosions and his teammates being blown to bits... Fucking A, he hated those.

When Matt joined them, Logan steered the couple toward the string of cabins left of the lodge. The ones on the right had filled up earlier. Serenity wasn't very big, although when all the cabins were rented, the place kept him and his brother running.

As they entered the end cabin, Logan flipped on the light switch and saw the young lady take in the accommodations. The king-size bed boasted a blue and gold quilt in a Texas-star pattern if he remembered correctly. Two nightstands and a dresser. A tiny woodstove in the corner. Two overstuffed armchairs with lamps. A small round table under the back window. A blue and green rag rug crocheted by Aunt Marg. Small bathroom in the back. Seriously rustic. He glanced at the city girl.

She looked a bit taken aback, then walked over to the bed and ran a hand down the quilt. "That's amazing how the colors shouldn't blend, but they do. Whoever made this has quite an eye."

"I'll tell my aunt Laverne you said so."

Matt sauntered in and dropped his suitcase beside the door before joining Rebecca. He wrapped an arm around her shoulders and nuzzled her neck. "Come hang out, babe."

She stiffened slightly and glanced at Logan, as if uncomfortable with public affection.

He smothered a grin. She was definitely hanging with the wrong crowd.

She stepped out of Matt's grasp. "I'm pretty beat."

Matt hesitated, his gaze going from Rebecca, then to the door, as if pulled by a magnet. "If you're sure…"

"I'm sure."

"Okay." He took a step toward the door and stopped. "Oh, the woodstove…"

"I'll show her," Logan said. He set her suitcase beside the other.

"Thanks, Logan. I'll be back soon, babe." Matt hurried out of the cabin as if afraid someone would stop him.

Somebody wanted to start swinging tonight, didn't he? With a cynical smile, Logan motioned the abandoned innocent over to the iron stove and knelt to put in kindling and logs from the adjacent bin. She stood close enough that her hip brushed against his shoulder. A soft, round hip. As he lit the fire and adjusted the vent, her fragrance wrapped around him. Her light soap smelled nice enough, but the underlying scent of sheer female made him want to strip her down and see if she tasted as sweet. He cleared his throat and shifted away. "Is all that clear?"

She frowned at the stove, studying it as if it were some esoteric puzzle he'd be quizzing her on later, then nodded. "I think I've got it. Thank you." To his relief and regret, she walked over to the tiny bookcase near the bed. As he rose to his feet, she pulled out a book with a happy cry. "*Little Women!* I haven't read this since grade school."

When her eyes lit up like that, she lost the city stuffiness and just looked appealing. Too appealing. Those pink lips went past kissable and edged into carnal.

"How late can I sleep in? Are there certain times for meals or some such?" she asked, holding the book like a precious treasure.

"Your group usually rotates cooking and KP, but hot coffee and snacks are always available in the kitchen."

"I'll be one of those in for early coffee." She wrinkled her nose in a way that merged the tiny freckles. "I'm a caffeine addict."

"I'll see you then." Logan reached the door, stopped—pretty women were hell on a man's thinking processes—and pulled keys out of his pocket. "Here's your key. I'll give Matt his at the lodge."

She crossed the room. As she took the big, old-fashioned key, her dimple flashed. "Cool. You have an interesting place, Mr. Hunt."

"It's Logan." He ran a finger down her cheek, finding her skin as soft as it looked. *Dammit.* "Welcome to Serenity."

Chapter Two

Early the next day, Rebecca followed Matt down the tiny trail toward the lodge. Her steps crackled on the frost-covered ground, and her breath turned white in the frigid air. She shivered, wrapping her arms around her body. Wasn't it almost summer? When they reached the clearing, she stopped and stared. Under a deep blue sky, mountains piled higher and higher until reaching the tallest, snow-capped peak. Fog spotted the mountainsides, and a few white patches drifted lazily up into the sky, as if wakened by the sun. Aside from the murmur of voices in the lodge and the gurgle of a nearby stream, silence ruled. No roar of cars or screech of brakes, no planes, no shouting, no music. Everything seemed almost too stark, the colors too sharp, the sounds too naked.

"C'mon, babe." Matt stood on the porch, hand on the door. "Let's go."

"Right. Sorry." She trotted up to join him. They crossed the empty main room to where the club members already filled the long table in the dining room.

"Hold on a minute," Matt said to her, putting his arm around her waist to stop her just inside the rough-hewn door frame. "Hey, everybody," Matt said loudly and waited for the noise to die down. "Most of you met Rebecca last night. She's new to swinging, so give her time and introduce yourselves as we go along."

Under the barrage of eyes, Rebecca nodded her head politely and crossed the room with Matt. As they took seats near the middle of one long table, she tried to ignore the assessing looks from the men. But how the heck could she ignore the fact that strangers were sizing her up for sex, and in an entirely different way than in a club. Considering the purpose of this weekend, these men *knew* they'd get lucky, right?

Okay, Rebecca, she told herself. Get with the program. She had a relationship to salvage and inhibitions to lose. Her stomach tightened, and she took a mental step back. For now, how about just make friends and have fun? *Make friends; have fun. Piece of cake.*

As the members returned to their various conversations, she poured herself coffee. No one should be forced to be sociable before coffee. That was just cruel. Taking a sip, she looked the crowd over. Some cute guys here. One with black hair and intense brown eyes and a trim mustache. One sounded like a college professor. He might be fun to talk with. Mostly couples, although two women and one man were obviously together. Interesting.

Taking the dishes passed to her by a black-haired woman in her thirties, Rebecca helped herself to the scrambled eggs and sausage and took a bite.

Matt politely requested the bowl of fruit to be passed. He glanced at Rebecca's plate and leaned closer. "Wouldn't you rather have something lighter, hon? Remember you said you wanted to watch your weight."

Months ago, after being lectured by Mom on the dire fate awaiting a heavy woman in a relationship, Rebecca had made that comment. He had never forgotten. As the eggs turned tasteless in her mouth, she switched to calorie-free coffee. Sure, she could tell herself that she felt comfortable with her body, but whom was she fooling? The comfort lasted only until someone—like Matt—made clear he considered her fat.

Of course, he never said the *F* word. He just wanted her to improve her health: eat less, exercise more, and get as skinny as all the women at this table. But she already exercised religiously, and she didn't eat that much. Face it: her heritage was round, her body was round, and unless she went for surgery and starved constantly like her mother, she was going to stay round.

How would he react if she told him his dick was too small?

She pushed the plate away, her appetite gone. When she looked up, her eyes met Logan's. He leaned against the doorway to the kitchen, studying her like some specimen on a petri dish. Probably wondering what she was doing with these members of fitness anonymous.

A perky blonde jumped up from her chair and clapped her hands. "All right, everyone. I'm Ashley, and today we're hiking up to Rainbow Lake. Serena and Michelle are making sandwiches for us. It's a bit of a walk, so wear good footwear, remember to bring your daypacks, and don't forget sunscreen."

A hike sounded like fun. San Francisco parks didn't look anything like this wilderness.

Ashley continued, "Jenna and Brandy will handle supper tonight, with their men on cleanup duty. And then we have our meet and greet. We'll play some games to get to know each other, and then see where the evening goes." The blonde licked her full lips and gave everyone a long, slow look, earning hoots and howls from the crowd.

* * *

Why the hell hadn't Jake returned from San Francisco? Logan wondered, grinding his teeth at the constant magpielike chattering of the people on the trail. Two more miles to Rainbow Lake. A shame he couldn't get them to jog, but maybe if he sped up some, they wouldn't have the breath to talk.

Usually Jake handled the social crap, while Logan did repairs and maintenance. People in individual packages could be enjoyable, but crowds? He'd rather get shot in the head. He ran a finger down the scar on his face and snorted. *Again.*

Stepping up on an outcropping of granite, he eyed the line of people trudging up the switchbacks. No stragglers. The group appeared in pretty good shape. Even fancy Rebecca in her designer jeans and shapeless top had kept up.

In fact, she did more than keep up. As she walked beside her boyfriend, her green eyes sparkled with pleasure, alert to everything the forest offered. Logan had seen her spot a mule deer frozen in place, a hawk in a dive, and a tiny deer mouse. Each time her face lit with wonder. Her open enjoyment added to his, and he found himself checking the line more often than normal just to catch her reactions.

The sun was high overhead and unseasonably hot by the time the trail descended, leaving the pines behind. He led the group across a grass- and wildflower-filled meadow to the tiny mountain lake, clear and blue and damned cold. Granite slabs poked up through the wildflowers, glimmering in the sun. With yells of delight, people dropped their backpacks and stripped.

Logan enjoyed the show of bare asses and breasts as the swingers splashed into the water like a herd of lemmings, screaming at the cold. As he leaned on a boulder, he noticed one person still completely dressed with wide eyes and open mouth. The city girl. Considering she and Matt bunked together, Rebecca couldn't be a virgin, but from her reaction, she was pretty innocent when it came to kink.

"C'mon, babe," her boyfriend yelled, already buck naked in the lake. "The water's great." Not waiting for her response, he waded out deeper, heading for a blonde who looked as if she had substituted bouncy breasts for cheerleading pom-poms.

Rebecca glanced from the water to the trail, back to the water, where Matt wrestled with Ashley, and back to the trail again.

Logan could see the exact moment she decided to leave. He walked over to block her way.

"Excuse me," she said politely.

"No."

Red surged into her cheeks, and her eyes narrowed as she glared at him. Red-gold hair. Freckles. Big bones. Looked like she had Irish ancestry and the temper to go with it. Stepping sideways to block her again, Logan tucked his thumbs into his front pockets and waited for the explosion.

"Listen, Mr. Hunt—"

"It's Logan," he interrupted and tried not to grin as her mouth compressed.

"Whatever. I'm going back to my cabin. Please move your... Please move."

"Sorry, sugar, but no one hikes alone. That's one safety rule I take seriously." He glanced at the swingers. "I can't leave them, and you can't walk alone, so you're stuck here."

Her eyes closed, and he saw the iron control she exerted over her emotions.

The Dom in him wondered how quickly he could break through that control to the woman underneath. Tie her up, tease her a bit, and watch her struggle not to give in to her need and... Hell, talk about inappropriate thoughts.

He pulled in a breath to cool off. No use. It was blistering hot, and not just from his visions of steamy sex. Nothing like global warming in the mountains. He frowned when he noted her damp face and the sweat soaking her long-sleeved, heavy shirt. Not good. The woman needed to get her temperature down.

At the far end of the meadow, the forest would provide shade. He could send her there to sit and cool off, but she'd be out of sight, and from the obstinate set of that pretty, pink mouth, she'd head right back down the trail in spite of his orders.

Shoulders straight, chin up, feet planted. Definitely a rebellious one, the type that brought his dominant nature to the fore. He'd love to give her an order and have her disobey, so he could enjoy the hell out of paddling that soft ass. But she wasn't his to discipline, more's the pity, since a woman like this was wasted on that pretty boy.

And he'd gotten sidetracked.

With a sigh, he returned to the problem at hand. She needed to stay here where he could keep an eye on her, and she needed to cool off.

"Even if you don't strip down completely, at least take some clothes off and wade in the water," he said. "You're getting overheated."

"Thank you, but I'm fine," she said stiffly.

"No, you're not." When he stepped closer, he felt the warmth radiating off her body. Being from San Francisco, she wouldn't be accustomed to the dryness or the heat. "Either strip down, little rebel, or I'll toss you in with your clothes on."

Her mouth dropped open.

He wouldn't, would he? Rebecca stared up at the implacable, cold eyes, seeing the man's utter self-confidence. Definitely not bluffing.

Well, he could be as stern as he wanted. Damned if she'd take her clothing off and display her chunky, scarred legs.

She shook her head, backing away. If she needed to, she'd run.

Faster than she could blink, he grabbed her arm.

She tugged and got nowhere. "Listen, you can't—"

With one hand, he unbuttoned her heavy shirt, not at all hindered by her efforts to shove his hand away. After a minute, her shirt flapped open, revealing her bra and her pudgy stomach. "Damn you!"

She glanced at the lake, hoping for Matt to rescue her, and froze. He was kissing the oh-so-perky Ashley, and not just a peck on the lips but a full clinch and deep-throating tongues. Rebecca stared as shock swept through her, followed by a wave of humiliation. He... As her breath hitched, she tore her gaze away, blinking against the welling tears. Why had she ever come here?

"Oh, sugar, don't do that now." Logan pulled her up against his chest, ignoring her weak protest. His arms held her against chest muscles hard as the granite outcroppings, and he turned so she couldn't see the lake. Silently, he stroked a hand down her back while she tried to pull herself together.

Matthew and Ashley would have sex. Soon. Somehow she hadn't quite understood the whole concept of swinging and what her gut-level reaction would be. But she could take it now that she realized...what would happen. After drawing in a shaky breath, she firmed her lips. Fine.

And if Logan insisted she strip to bra and panties, that was fine too. So what if these people saw her giant thighs and ugly scars. She'd never see any of them again. Ever.

For a second, she let herself enjoy the surprising comfort of Logan's arms. Then she pushed away.

He let her take a step back and then grasped her upper arms, keeping her in place as he studied her face.

She flushed and looked away. God, how embarrassing. She had melted down in front of a total stranger, showing him exactly how insecure she was. But he'd been nice, and she owed him. "Thank you for...uh...the shoulder."

With a finger, he turned her face back to him. "I like holding you, Rebecca. Come to me anytime you need a shoulder." A crease appeared in his cheek. He ran his finger across the skin at the top of her lacy bra, his finger slightly rough, sending unexpected tingles through her. "You think I can talk you out of this too?"

The thought of being braless led to her imagining his big hands touching her breasts, how all his strength could hold her in place, and... *God, get a grip, Rebecca.* She shook her head and stepped back hastily.

He eyed her, and his look heated her more than the noon sun. "You will, at least, strip down to bra and briefs." One corner of his mouth tipped up. "If you don't, I'll do it for you. And I'll enjoy every minute."

Her insides turned to molten lava. How could she be appalled at his threat and excited at the same time? "Fine. But I'll take my own clothes off," she said, her mouth dry. She shrugged her shirt off.

"I'd almost rather lose," he murmured and tugged a lock of her hair before striding away. Closer to the water, he resumed lifeguard duty, turning his back to her. Thank God.

Her fingers clumsy, she managed to get her boots and jeans off. After a bracing breath, dressed only in her best pink underwear, she hurried toward the water. She passed him, horribly conscious of how the bright sun revealed her body's every flaw and jiggle and scar.

Ignoring the shock of the coldness, she waded out until the concealing water came up to her shoulders.

"Hey, Rebecca joined us!" The crowd swarmed her way with welcoming yells. With only her head and arms exposed, she relaxed enough to join in the play, splashing and dunking with the rest. After the first few times, she ignored the men's roving hands. Unfortunately, the touching didn't excite her in the least. Maybe because the men didn't even know her. To them, she was just another available female, another set of breasts and bottom.

Logan, at least, had really looked at her. And the look he'd given her had aroused her more than being touched by the others. Unable to resist, she glanced over her shoulder. He still leaned against the rock, arms crossed over his broad chest. His gaze was cool. Impersonal.

Good. That was good. No attraction there. Good. She turned back around and dodged Paul's hand.

The icy water precluded swimming for long. While the others rummaged through their packs for lunch, Rebecca yanked on her clothes and then grabbed her own food. Everyone scattered, perching here and there on the warm rocks to eat. Matt joined Rebecca, slinging an arm around her as if nothing had happened. As they cheerfully argued the role of women in the gold rush, she remembered why she'd dated him in the first place. Smart, polite, charming, and darned good-looking, especially now with the sun gleaming on his blond hair and brightening his blue eyes. Her perfect man. Surely they could work things out. Yes, they'd be—

"Hey, you two. I brought dessert." Balancing a plate, Ashley crowded onto the slab of rock on Matt's other side. "Here, try this." She fed Matt a bite of chocolate cake, giggling when he nipped her fingers.

Rebecca's hand closed into a fist. One good punch, and the big-breasted blonde would go ass over teakettle. But Ashley only did what they'd come here for. Rebecca turned her head, pretending to concentrate on Paul and Amy's conversation, trying to ignore Matt's husky laughter. Her chest tightened, making swallowing impossible, so she rolled up the remains of her sandwich.

Putting it into her pack gave her an excuse to move away from Ashley and Matt. She pulled out her sketch pad. There, she'd have an excuse to stay apart.

It didn't take long for the magic of drawing to assert itself, and she lost herself in the subtleties of lines and curves and shadows. She did a small line drawing of Brandy's bare toes digging in the dirt, her hiking boots and socks nearby. Another quick one of Christopher reclining on a granite slab, reminding her of the models who posed nude during art classes.

After a while, she glanced back at Matt and saw Ashley's hand creep between his legs. *Okay, then. That's how it's going to be.* She averted her gaze and saw Logan.

Slightly apart from the group, he leaned on a rock, eating his lunch. He'd removed his shirt, and good Lord but working around a lodge made for some serious muscles. The brown hair on his chest was a shade darker than his skin, an inverted triangle going from nipple to nipple and down. She couldn't see any tan lines on his arms. Either he worked with his shirt off or lay out naked. And wasn't that a thought? She slid her gaze past his six-pack abdomen to the waist of his jeans. No flash of paler skin showed, so he... Oops. Startling blue eyes in a tanned face trapped her gaze, holding her frozen. The ground under her dropped an inch, a foot, sliding inexorably out from under her as he studied her.

When his eyes released her, she almost fell backward.

Chapter Three

After supper, the club members took over the big lodge room, shoving chairs and couches into the center of the room. When Matt took a seat on one couch and tugged Rebecca down beside him, she frowned at him. Although he'd been attentive enough on the hike down the mountain and since then, resentment still burned inside her chest.

Get over it, girl. He hasn't done anything wrong, after all. Swinging, remember? They'd come to screw other people, and she needed to get with the program. She gave him a sidelong look. Maybe she'd just screw everything and everyone in sight. Plastering a sweet smile on her face, she asked, "So what happens now?"

He patted her hand. "This is a 'meet and greet,' where we play games to break the ice."

She settled back on the couch and sipped her wine. *Fine.* God knew she'd done enough of this sort of thing during team-building exercises. They'd probably start with a stand-up-and-tell—

"Rebecca," Mel said, interrupting her thoughts. His T-shirt curved over his round belly as he pointed at her. "Stand up and tell us something about you."

As everyone turned to look at her, she stood. Just like giving a presentation to a client. "My name is Rebecca, and I'm an artist in an advertising firm. This is the first time I've been out of the city, and the first time I've done...swinging stuff...so I'm feeling somewhat lost."

The expressions of sympathy and welcome comforted her. These were nice people. Really. So maybe she was just too uptight, like Matt said, and she should give them a chance. She'd come here for exactly that, right? To explore her sexuality and get in touch with her inner vamp. To keep her perfect relationship intact.

After the formalities, the couples split apart, joining different groups to play games. Matt chose the group playing Twister, and Rebecca watched for a few minutes. Whoever fell over had to take off clothing, and one petite brunette deliberately lost her balance at least twice.

"Rebecca, join us." Brandon grabbed her hand and pulled her off the couch. On the other side of the room, Ginger sat beside Paul, the college professor, and Christopher by Serena. Rebecca took a seat beside Brandon.

Motioning toward the coffee table set up with dice, a board game, and a pile of cards, Ginger said, "Okay, gang. Roll the dice and move your marker. Do whatever the space you land on says. If you win a card, you give it to someone, and that person has to do what it says. If you roll doubles, you have to remove an article of clothing." She assumed a severe expression. "Jewelry doesn't count as clothing."

"Wahoo," Brandon said, rubbing his hands together. "Let's get started."

Rebecca sucked in a breath. She could do this.

As the game progressed, Ginger had to remove her shirt and bra. Christopher lost his shoes. Paul, his socks.

Rebecca landed on a square and read the command. "Oh God." Paul laughed and filled her wineglass. She drank it down and took her shirt off. For the second time today.

On his turn, Brandon drew a card and then handed it to her. "Read it aloud."

"Stand up and give the person a French kiss. All body parts should touch." *Good grief.*

He rose to his feet and waggled his fingers in a come-here gesture.

I can do this—her own personal mantra, at least in *this* place. Rebecca put her hands on his shoulders. Not very muscular. Nice cologne. His hands spread over her bare back as he pulled her closer, until her breasts squashed against his chest. She kissed him. His mouth was wet, his mustache tickled, and his tongue technique lacked finesse. She wrapped her arms around him tighter, trying to feel something erotic. Surely she shouldn't be critiquing during a hot kiss.

But it just wasn't that hot. In the past, she'd occasionally stuck out as the only sober one in a drunken crowd; this time, she was the only frigid one in a horny crowd.

She drank more wine.

Faces became flushed. Voices louder and sillier. One couple moved to a couch farther away to make out. Michelle and Greg quit playing Twister and stripped down in front of the fire. Within a minute, Greg lay flat, Michelle straddling him and guiding his penis into her.

Good grief. Rebecca turned her eyes away. The patterns of the room had changed. And she didn't see Matt anywhere.

Her turn with the dice. She rolled a double. Ginger giggled, and the three men leaned forward expectantly, waiting for her to choose what she'd take off.

"Take your bra off, honey." Brandon put his hand on her breast as if she didn't understand.

Was this passion she felt? Hardly. *Rebecca's inner vamp has left the building.* She set her wine down, picked up her shirt, and rose. "Sorry, folks, but I guess I'm just not a swinger. I'm heading to bed." When Brandon stood up eagerly, she withered him with a cold stare. "Alone."

Others headed out in twos and threes, making their way to the cabins. As Rebecca went out the lodge door, she looked back. Three more had joined the two in front of the fire. Whoa, lots of naked body parts there. God, she so should not have come here. But how would she know unless she gave it a try, right? Obviously some people—including Matt—really enjoyed this…stuff.

A splatter of rain hit her naked shoulders as she stepped off the porch. Wind whipping at her hair, she tugged on her shirt, hurrying down the trail to the cabin. With a sigh of relief, she unlocked the door and flicked on the light.

"Hey!" Matt's voice. He reclined on the bed, naked; Ashley knelt between his legs, her mouth fastened to his cock.

Rebecca gasped. A sick wail ballooned inside her head, ringing in her ears, although nothing escaped her throat.

Ashley didn't release him, just looked over and smirked. Her head slowly bobbed up and down.

"C'mere, babe," Matt said, motioning with his free hand. The other massaged Ashley's breast. "You can join us. I like getting it on with two women."

Rebecca took a step back and found her voice from wherever it had gone. "I don't think I'd enjoy it. Sorry, Matt. And sorry for the interruption." She backed up, telling herself not to be petty by slamming the door.

She slammed the door so hard that pinecones pattered onto the ground from the closest trees.

Petty is as petty does. But that was her perfect boyfriend in their cabin. With Ashley and her fat lips around his cock. The porch step blurred, and Rebecca tripped, landing on her hands and knees. Grit burned into her hands, and her eyes stung with tears. She blinked furiously. Damned if she'd cry.

She staggered to her feet, her head spinning. She'd drank too much alcohol trying to fit in. Hadn't worked, had it? Standing in the rain, she wiped the tears from her eyes and water from her face. "Damn, damn, damn." Where could she find a bed tonight? Feeling like she was stuck on a merry-go-round, she headed back to the lodge. Once there, she peeked inside. In front of the fire, people roiled together like a massive animal with way too many arms and legs. She backed out quickly.

She sure couldn't sleep in there. Maybe the kitchen? No. The moron who built the oversize doorways for the dining room and kitchen had somehow neglected to include actual doors. With her luck, some male idiot looking for wine would trip over her instead. No way.

Staring down the trails, she saw people coming and going from the cabins in a raunchy version of musical chairs. *Musical cabins?* But she was the loser, the one left without a chair. Or bed. *Fine. Who needs a bed anyway?*

Scowling, she walked over to the porch swing. Pulling her wet shirt tighter, she curled up on the damp cushions. In the shadows, no one would see her, and she might be cold, but at least she'd be free of wandering hands and wet lips. She shuddered, cutting off that train of thought. Had she really wanted a relationship with Matt so badly?

Her mother's psychiatrist husband would probably call it a life lesson. *And how.*

* * *

Logan opened the lodge door to go inside and paused when Thor whined behind him. Had a mouse or rat holed up under the porch? "What is it, boy?"

When the dog nosed the porch swing, Logan walked over. "Well, hell." Rebecca lay on the cushions, curled into a ball and shivering. Before making his rounds, he'd watched her down a fair amount of wine. Was she drunk?

He touched her neck and winced. Too cold. Worry turned his mouth down. "You, woman, are a pain in the ass," he muttered and scooped her up.

As he carried her over to the door leading upstairs, he saw at a glance why she hadn't come inside. Busy people, these swingers. He noted with appreciation the brunette's legs-up position. And the blonde's bare pussy wasn't bad either.

After he punched in the code on the keypad, he climbed the stairs to his quarters and opened the door without dropping the city girl. He deserved a prize, but the half-conscious woman wasn't going to be handing them out. Not tonight.

He flipped on a light, made his way past his living room, his small kitchen, and into the bedroom. As he laid her on the bed, he grinned. Looked like he got to strip her after all.

Her shirt pulled over her head easily enough. With reluctance, he left her lacy blue bra on. Nice underwear, but he ached to fill his hands with her full breasts. He didn't. How about that? Chivalry wasn't completely dead.

Getting off her wet shirt revived her enough that she batted at his hands when he pulled her jeans off, but the alcohol and cold had left her only half-conscious. Not good. Her soggy jeans landed with a *splat* on the hardwood floor. Logan groaned as the dim light from the living room turned her pale thighs into an erotic dream against his dark red quilt. Dammit, he'd really like to wrap those legs around his waist and... *Don't go there*. He ran his fingers over the shadowy ridges of old scars on her calf, then pulled the quilt out from under her and tucked her in.

He eyed her. Hot drink first.

She roused to take some hot chocolate, although she wasn't especially polite. City girl had a mouth on her when riled. Setting the cup on the nightstand, Logan stripped and joined her. Rolling her onto her side, he pulled her back against his chest and molded her frozen little body against his. Skin to skin warmed a person quickly. God, she was soft.

She gave a low, husky sigh.

Christ help him, he bet she'd sound like that when a man entered her. Her soft ass nestled against his groin and against a cock so hard, even her chilled skin couldn't cool him off. Unable to resist, he pressed his lips against the curve of her shoulder. She smelled of only soap and woman. Considering her classy city clothing, he'd expected a fancy perfume.

And what was Miss Modesty doing with this troupe of swingers? The little rebel just didn't add up, and he wanted a few answers. Later. For now, he buried his face in her silky hair and cupped his hand over her breast. A man was entitled to some small pleasures when saving a woman's life, especially since her presence in his bed meant he'd have to stay awake. God help them both if he should fall asleep.

* * *

In the middle of the night, Rebecca woke draped over Matt, toasty warm and thoroughly confused. When had she returned to the cabin? She distinctly remembered freezing her butt off on the porch swing. Had he come back for her and put her into bed? Surely she hadn't had that much to drink.

She moved slightly and stiffened. Her cheek rested in the hollow of a man's shoulder, a very muscular shoulder. Her arm lay across a chest much broader than Matt's, and her fingers touched crisp hair. Matt's chest was bare as a teenage boy's.

No expensive cologne either, just the clean scent of soap and pine and...definitely man. A hard arm curved around her back, and the hand gripping her shoulder had callused fingers.

This isn't Matthew.

Had she gotten so drunk she'd gone to bed with one of the swingers? No, she couldn't have. She hadn't been that brainless since her college days when she discovered sex.

"You awake, sugar?"

Her mouth dropped open. The deep, raspy voice could belong to only one man. "Mr. Hunt."

The laugh rumbled through his chest like a minor earthquake. "Considering your position, perhaps you'd better call me Logan."

Her leg was tucked between his thighs, her knee pressing against his groin, and her thigh touching... Oh my, his chest wasn't the only body part bigger than Matt's, and he was fully aroused. A wave of heat washed through her, surely caused by embarrassment and not excitement. "How did I...? We didn't..."

Another rumbling laugh. "No, we didn't. I found you on the porch swing, and you were well on your way to hypothermia. I brought you up here and got in to warm you up." His hand stroked her upper arm, the touch firm. "But if you'd like to warm up even more, I'm willing."

"No, thanks." She tried to push away from him.

The arm around her back tightened, holding her in place. "Uh-uh. Your body temperature is still low, and I'm not going to have all my careful work ruined by you stomping back outside."

"I'll go back to my cabin and..." And what? God knew who might be in there now. The memory of Matt and Ashley curled inside her like a rotting worm. With a sigh, she gave up. "Never mind. I'll stay here."

"Good choice. Nothing's going to happen to you now; I prefer to bed women in full possession of their wits." She felt his lips touch the top of her head. "But in the morning, you might be in trouble."

Memo to self: remember to get up and out before dawn. The tenseness eased out of her muscles when he didn't try anything. She still had on her underwear, so he really hadn't taken advantage. When his hand stroked up and down her arm, more comforting than carnal, she let herself drift.

Logan waited until her breathing slowed, her muscles went lax, and she hovered on the edge of sleep. Time for interrogation, vanilla-style. Yeah, rope would be a hell of a lot more fun. "Why are you with the swingers?"

Drowsily, she rubbed her cheek against his chest, hardening him to discomfort. "Matt wanted me to come. Thought it would make our sex life..." Her words trailed off into a yawn.

The idea of her boyfriend being inadequate to her needs made Logan grin. "It doesn't bother you he's with other women?"

The whimper she gave broke his heart. Yes, it bothered her. Her fingers toyed with the hair on his chest and then went still. Her brain had disengaged again.

"He's a jerk?"

"He's perfect. Just...I...no swinger." Her hand languidly stroked the muscles on his shoulder. "...doesn't like my body."

"Mmmph." Logan had to grit his teeth to keep from rolling over and driving into the body Matt didn't like. If anything could snap his control, it would be a soft, round woman pressed against him. "Not everybody likes skinny women, Becca."

"Daddy did."

Logan frowned. Sometimes the present-day culture didn't make much sense, especially in its inability to appreciate lush women. This little one should have been born a few decades ago, when she could have given Marilyn Monroe some competition.

Her breathing slowed even further, her hand going limp on his shoulder, which was a pity. He'd been wondering how he could entice those sleepy fingers to explore farther down. With his free hand, he ran his knuckles over her soft cheek.

Matt was an idiot.

Chapter Four

Rebecca's internal alarm went off a while before dawn. As she opened her eyes, she realized their positions had shifted during the night, so now she lay on her back with him pressed against her side. One of his hands cupped her breast, and even through her bra, the feel of his fingers sent a thrill through her. How weird. How wrong. She hated Matt's behavior with Ashley, and now she wondered what it would be like to make love with Logan.

Hypocrite. Then again, her relationship with Matt probably wouldn't survive this weekend, she realized with an aching pain. Nonetheless, getting out of this bed would be a clever idea. Ever so carefully, she moved Logan's hand and started to inch out from under his arm.

"I'm awake, sugar, so all those maneuvers aren't necessary." His hand slid back to take possession of her breast again, this time easing under her bra to her bare skin. At the rough caress of his fingers, her nipple bunched up, and a spike of arousal shot straight to her core.

"Well, now," he murmured, his thumb circling her nipple.

"Listen, I don't want—"

"No, your problem is that you *do* want." He rolled over, and his weight flattened her into the bed. And *oh*, he felt incredibly good. She could feel her panties turn damp. Nudging her legs apart, he settled his hips between her thighs.

"Logan," she whispered, "no." She pushed against a chest as solid as a boulder, and as unmovable.

"Becca, yes. You owe me a good-morning kiss at least." He added in a mock-serious voice, "I saved your life, you know. You could well have died out there."

The faint light from another room played over his beard-shadowed jaw. Lines radiated out from the corners of his eyes, crinkling as she stared up at him. His erection pressed against the juncture of her legs, the only barrier her thin panties. When her hands splayed against his chest, the crisp hair couldn't disguise the rock-hard muscles beneath.

As before, coming up against his massive body, she felt feminine and soft and very tempted. "A kiss? No more."

"It's a start." He dipped his head to the curve where her neck met her shoulder. The arousing contrast of his velvety lips and the scratch of his morning beard wakened a flutter deep in her belly.

Her hands clutched his wide shoulders, and she didn't know whether to pull him closer or push him away. She shouldn't do this.

He solved the question by moving to her mouth, rumbling a laugh when she kept it closed. A sharp nip on her lower lip made her gasp, and his tongue plunged within. His kiss was skilled, experienced…and overwhelming.

The demanding thrust of his tongue made her think of other places he could be thrusting. Each time he moved, his cock bumped against her pussy, each touch like a spark of sensation. Her fingers tightened on his shoulders as she tried to find her eroding balance.

His hand stroked her breast, his palm so big he could hold her fully. When he sucked her tongue into his mouth, an ache of need burned through her body. Slow, thorough, he kissed her forever, and by the time he raised his head, her fingers were buried in his thick hair.

Propping himself on an elbow, he fondled her breast. "When you took your shirt off yesterday, I had trouble keeping my hands off," he murmured. His fingers circled her nipple and then rolled the peak. His eyes on her face, he increased the pressure until sparks shot down to her sex, and her lower half went liquid. The gentle stroke of his thumb eased the throbbing, and then he moved to her other breast.

Oh God, he knew exactly what he was doing, painting her like a canvas, each stroke deepening the intensity. "Logan," she whispered, shivering as unfamiliar sensations rushed through her.

His hand stilled, pressing against her breast and holding her still as he studied her. "Too much?" he asked softly.

"I don't..." God, her body was flaming out of control, and she wanted his hands all over her. Wanted him inside her with an intensity she hadn't felt before.

No. She didn't have sex with strangers. She pulled in a breath, and the scent of him made her head spin.

"It's all right, Becca." His next kiss was softer, less demanding, his hand on her breast gentled. Her body edged back into her control as the need died back to a simmer. A relief, but a tad disappointing. Her breathing slowed.

Leaning back, he regarded her with steel blue eyes. After a second, the intense gaze made her feel vulnerable. She started to sit up.

His hand between her breasts flattened her like a pancake, sending her pulse spiking. A thrill of excitement rippled through her body, and his eyes narrowed. "Not as vanilla as you look, are you?" His hand didn't let up, keeping her pressed into the mattress.

Her voice came out shaky. "What do you mean?"

His slow grin made her pulse stutter. Still between her legs, he grasped her hands and raised her arms over her head. Clasping her wrists with one big hand, he anchored them above the pillow.

"Hey." She struggled, and his grip tightened. Arms stretched above her head, his weight on her hips... She couldn't move. Fear swirled through her, accompanied by a startling wave of heat. "Let me go." Her voice came out husky.

"You want me to?" With his free hand, he shoved her bra up, and the elastic band caught on the rigid peaks of her nipples. He ran his finger around one puckered areola, then the other, and somehow they tightened even further. Her breath caught as pleasure rushed through her.

His fingers played with her breasts as his blue eyes focused on her face. "Just look at you," he murmured. "All confused and excited." His voice deepened. "You know, little rebel, with your hands restrained, I can do anything I want to you."

Instinctively, she struggled. She got nowhere; his grip was unyielding, his strength immense. And each useless try shot another current of excitement through her, until her pussy ached with need. Panting, she stared up into his intense gaze.

He chuckled, then pushed her breast upward so he could take it in his mouth. Hot. Wet.

She moaned. The sound shocked her. What was she doing? She didn't even know him.

When she strained against his grip on her hands, he bit down carefully on her nipple. The sharp pain sizzled straight to her clit, hitting with a shock that made her clench inside. Oh God. She was drowning in sensation. In heat.

He licked the distended peak, his tongue hot; his breath cooled her skin, and then he bit again. Her back arched uncontrollably, pushing her breasts upward.

"Very nice, little rebel," he murmured, switching to the other breast until both were swollen, her nipples tight and aching. When he sat back on his knees, she managed to breathe again. At least until she saw his gaze move down her body. Thank God the light was dim, but unfortunately not nearly enough to hide the size of her hips. Why did he have to see—

"I'm going to owe you a pair of briefs," he said, breaking into her thoughts. Taking hold of her panties, he ripped one side, then the other, and tossed the destroyed fabric onto the floor.

"Hey!" she said indignantly, despite the thrill coursing through her at his action. Then she realized...if his hands were there, her arms weren't pinned any longer. She yanked her arms down and tried to sit up. He put a hand in the middle of her chest and pushed her back down. With a quick one-two movement, he snatched her wrists, clamping them in one hand again, resting them on her stomach.

He studied her for a moment, his free hand caressing one breast. "You're not ready for me to take you," he murmured. "But we'll go a bit further down this path."

Keeping her hands anchored to her stomach, he edged downward between her thighs. When he leaned sideways, he trapped her left leg under his waist. He propped himself up on his right elbow, using the same hand to restrain her wrists. With his knee, he pushed her right leg out.

"What are you doing?" She squirmed, all too aware of how he'd wedged her legs open. Her underwear was gone, her pussy unshielded.

"I'm pleasing myself, sugar. I like seeing a woman open and vulnerable," he said, his gaze running down her body, stopping at the juncture of her legs. "But if you're not interested in continuing, we'll stop right now."

His free hand slid down over her mound and touched her folds, then pressed against the betraying wetness. *Oh God.* She closed her eyes against the amusement in his face.

"That feels like interest to me," he murmured. With one finger, he stroked down between her labia and back up to circle her clit. Each circuit increased the throbbing of the nerves there, and she could feel how engorged it was. His finger never slowed, never went faster. Never touched the nub where the need was most intense.

A thin whine escaped her, and her hips lifted.

"You can't push me to go faster, little one." He gave a deep laugh. "In fact, you can't do anything at all; I'm going to finger fuck you until you come."

Her breath caught at his words pointing out her helplessness. She strained against his powerful grip, and her inability to move started a shaking deep inside. She'd hated when Matt asked her for directions. This man wasn't asking at all, just telling her. Not even letting her move. As if her vulnerability had been the spark, her blood flamed through her veins.

"No," she whispered. This was so wrong.

"Yes," he whispered back. When she yanked again, he pushed a finger into her vagina, hard and fast. She gasped. The excruciating shot of pleasure devastated her senses, making her head spin. Her swollen labia throbbed as his finger slid in and out in a ruthless rhythm, until her vagina pulsed with him, until her insides tightened around the intrusion.

He didn't stop.

He added another finger, and she moaned. Even as the pleasure increased, the pressure built inside her, the intensity frightening. Her hips lifted, trying for more. Her legs quivered, straining against his unyielding body.

His thumb skated over her clit, gliding directly over it each time his fingers plunged into her. One stroke, and another and another. Her body coiled tighter and tighter as the burning torment continued.

When he paused, she moved—tried to move—only her wrists were trapped in his inflexible grip. She couldn't do anything, couldn't move.

His thumb rolled over her clit, and the climax exploded inside her like fireworks in the dark, blinding and deafening. Her hips bucked uncontrollably against his hand as a maelstrom of pleasure tore through her.

His fingers in her milked each spasm out; every flicker of his thumb over her clit sent another surge of ecstasy through her until she couldn't bear any more.

"Stop." When she lifted her head, his fingers pressed deeper into her, and her head dropped back weakly.

"Oh, not quite yet," he murmured. "You have another quiver or two in you." His thumb brushed featherlight over the oversensitive nub. Her vagina clenched and rippled around his fingers.

He did it again.

"God," she moaned.

He chuckled, easing his fingers out, and even that made her shudder. Still holding her wrists, he slid up beside her. "Very nice. I like that dazed look." Putting his hand along her jaw, he tilted her head and took her mouth hard. Her head started to spin again.

And suddenly her hands were free. She blinked and looked up into his hard face.

His lips curved as he stroked his thumb over her cheek. "Damn, you're tempting." With a sigh, he rolled over and swung out of bed.

Her body chilled without his warmth next to her, and she felt bare inside, as if he'd stolen her confidence. What had she done? She didn't know him, and she'd let him hold her down. Touch her.

Make her come more strongly than she'd ever come. She closed her eyes and took a couple of deep breaths. *Don't think about that.* She'd had an interesting night and played around some. That's all this had been. And now it was morning and over.

Frowning at the shadowy ridges on her legs, she dragged the blankets to her chest. He must not have noticed her scars, thank God. She sat up, trying to ignore the limp feel of her muscles.

Over at a chest of drawers, Logan pulled out jeans and a shirt, totally unselfconscious about being naked. He looked even bigger without clothing on. All powerful muscle and a very large erection.

Guilt sliced through her. He'd given her an orgasm like she'd dreamed about, and she'd given him nothing. The thought of having his hands on her again made her nervous. Excited. *Worried.* How far would she go if he touched her again? But fair was fair. She'd gotten off, and he hadn't. "What about you?"

Obviously seeing her gaze on his cock, he walked back over to the bed. His blue eyes crinkled. "You have a soft heart, don't you? But we're done, Becca. I pushed your limits enough for one day."

As he turned from her, she couldn't seem to find her voice, if she could have figured out what to say anyway.

He pulled on the jeans—commando—and a blue flannel shirt. "I'm going to let Thor out and do a quick check of the grounds. You've got time for a shower if you want to take one here. I doubt anyone else will be up for a bit."

She knew he'd made the offer so she wouldn't have to go back to her cabin and see Matt with Ashley. The thoughtfulness made her eyes swim with tears. "Thank you. That's very nice of you."

His grin was devastating, and she realized she hadn't seen him really smile before. He loomed over her and took her face between his big hands. "I've been called many things, but never nice. And if I see you all soft and pink in my bed much longer, I'm going to push you onto your back and take you in every way I can think of. So I'm leaving while I still can."

His words and the image of him...taking...what he wanted heated her skin faster than a sauna. He tilted her head back and possessed her mouth instead. Deeply. Thoroughly.

The door closed behind him before she'd caught her breath.

Thor at his side, Logan stalked down the trail to the cabins. The freezing mountain air needed to work more quickly; his jeans were past uncomfortable and well into painful. He should have left before that last kiss.

But turning away at that point had been fucking impossible. The blankets she'd clasped had plumped up her full breasts and revealed the soft curve of her shoulders. Pale shoulders with tantalizing freckles. And her mouth had been pink and wet and swollen from his kisses. Christ have mercy, but what would those lips feel like around his cock?

Hell. He kicked a dead branch off the trail and increased his pace. *Do not even consider taking her to bed.*

She had a man already.

Not a good deterrent, he realized. Too tempting to snatch her away from the idiot. He needed a better reason to avoid her.

First reason: She was a city girl. Big turn-off. Look at her clothes. Wore a suit to a mountain lodge. Designer jeans. She didn't even own hiking shoes. From the look on her face yesterday, she'd never visited a mountain before, let alone a forest. Hell, she probably exercised on a treadmill in an air-conditioned health club rather than outdoors.

She lived in a city, and he had to live in the mountains. His nightmares ensured that, and ensured he'd sleep alone and stay alone. Even now, he felt the lack of sleep over the past two nights drag at him.

Aside from the physical attraction, they had nothing in common.

His mouth twisted into a wry grin. Pretty worthless deterrent considering that when he went to Dark Haven in San Francisco, he had no trouble thoroughly enjoying the city girls. And being a guy, he wouldn't blow off a nice physical attraction anyway. He'd enjoyed the hell out of having her warm, curvy body up against his all night and wouldn't mind repeating it a time or two, even if he had to go without sleep.

Unfortunately, he wouldn't be content to just hold her again. Not after having his fingers in her little wet pussy. He shook his head, remembering how her forest green eyes had watched him dress and then puddled up because he'd been *nice* to her. Hell, if she knew the dark things he wanted to do to her, she'd run screaming down the mountain.

He snorted, thinking of how he'd hidden the cuffs chained to the head- and footboards under the mattress. Would she have panicked if she'd found them? Probably.

Although many normal women enjoyed acting out a rape fantasy like this morning, real submission terrified them.

But what if Rebecca possessed more guts than the others? More daring? He envisioned restraining her arms over her head, securing the cuffs tightly enough that her breasts would arch up. Of teasing those soft pink nipples until she... Like hell. Shy, modest Rebecca indulge in kink? Not gonna happen.

And although he might play at vanilla sex a time or two, he wanted more. Needed more. And could easily get more. A competent Dom rarely lacked for partners. Yet he couldn't help but wonder what Rebecca's whimpers would sound like if he tied her down and teased her until she begged for release.

He scowled. She'd better stay away from him. If she didn't, he'd teach her things the swingers had never thought of.

* * *

Rebecca showered and dressed, wrinkling her nose at having to put on yesterday's clothing. Matt had better have that blonde...person gone by after breakfast or she'd pound the door in.

Coffee. She needed coffee before her brain would work. And she definitely needed caffeine before she thought about last night and this morning. Matthew. Logan. Sex.

Need coffee...

She walked down the stairs and checked the lodge. Someone—probably Logan—had built the fire up, and the warmth radiated through the room. Only three people remained, twined together on the biggest couch. The man lifted his head at the sound of Rebecca's soft footsteps, then shook the women on top of him. "You two are supposed to make breakfast, remember?"

"Hell with that. I'm sleeping in," one woman said.

"If I try to cook, I'll puke, dammit," the other woman whined. "Why did you let me drink so much last night?"

"Like I could stop you?" The man's head dropped back onto the arm of the couch. Sighs, grumbles, and then silence.

Shaking her head, Rebecca headed for the kitchen. Empty. She started the coffeemaker, leaning on the counter for support until she could coax a cupful out, then burned her mouth on the first few gulps. As the caffeine began to work, it seemed as if the world brightened from muted tones to the full spectrum of life as her brain sparked to life. No matter what historians claimed, BC really stood for "Before Coffee."

After drinking another cup, she surveyed the possibilities for breakfast. The fridge held pounds of bacon, cartons of eggs, and butter. Potatoes in a bin. Flour and salt in a cupboard. She hadn't cooked for more than two people since her job during college, but no one forgot how to scramble eggs, and it gave her something useful to do.

And something to take her mind off last night. The memory of Logan's solid body seemed imprinted on hers. She scrubbed the potatoes and remembered how he'd pressed her into the mattress and kissed her, his cock jutting against her stomach. Would she have let him take her if he'd tried?

Her thighs pressed together over a suddenly throbbing clit. Why hadn't she been braver? *Or less brave?* If she'd been adamant about her refusal, he wouldn't have pushed, and she wouldn't feel so...sleazy and very embarrassed. And hot.

Dammit, why couldn't she have gotten interested in a swinger or two instead? They were not nearly as scary. What he'd done to her...pinning her arms down. The way he'd talked and watched her. She blew out a breath. Very exciting and very frightening in a way.

Finger fucked. What a term. And that was just what he'd done. Her insides quivered at the memory of his callused finger slick with her own wetness, sliding through her folds, pushing deep inside her. She had never come like that in her life. Ever. "*Stop,*" she'd told him, and "*Oh, not quite yet,*" he'd answered and just kept doing what he wanted with her body.

Matt's constant asking what she wanted in bed had annoyed her. Logan didn't ask, and her body loved it. That was absolutely the most frightening thing about this whole matter. She'd never considered herself a needy woman or a pushover, but she sure acted that way with him. So where did that leave her?

The sex...okay, totally awesome. The man...gorgeous. The possible consequences...not to be borne. No more messing around with Logan. If she wanted to explore kinky sex, she should practice on one of the good-looking swingers. One of the very available swingers.

She set the potato down in the sink and stared out the window at the surrounding forest. They were available, she repeated to herself. Available and all too willing to screw any woman in the place. Knowing that pretty much killed any attraction for her. With a huff of a laugh, she picked up the potato and resumed scrubbing. *Monogamous "R" me.*

Shaking her head, she remembered the fantasy she'd had before agreeing to try this weekend. Now that she thought about it, her fantasy hadn't included a multitude of men, but just one. *Some man would come into her room. Maybe she would hesitate, and he'd grab her, pin her to the mattress, force her to cooperate.* She scowled. That sounded like her morning with Logan. So what did that say about her?

Don't want to swing; *do* want to be pushed around? She bit her lip. Talk about politically incorrect, especially for a feminist like her.

As she grated potatoes, she considered her options for the rest of the weekend and came to one conclusion. Matt would simply have to take her home. She couldn't tolerate staying another night, watching Matt messing around, and dodging the other men. She'd made a mistake. Big-time.

Her lips curved. But this morning made up for a lot, even if it left her unsettled. And damned confused. He'd restrained her hands; why should that make her so hot?

Home. Time to go home, Rebecca. A twinge of guilt ran through her. Such a long drive. By the time Matt had taken her home and returned back here, the day would be gone.

Nevertheless.

She put the potatoes on to fry and whipped up some drop biscuits before putting the bacon in the oven. She smiled as the fragrance filled the room.

Serena and Greg wandered into the kitchen, looking fairly cheerful.

"I'm starving," Greg said, shoving his wire-rims up on his nose. "I thought there'd be food by now. Weren't Ginger and Amy supposed to cook today?"

"They're a bit under the weather," Rebecca said lightly. "And I'm an early riser." She tucked the biscuits in the hot oven with a satisfaction that she hadn't felt in a long time. Cooking just for herself never seemed worth the bother.

After flipping the hash browns, she started cracking eggs. As she counted in her head, she heard something scratch at the back door and then a low whine. The eggshell shattered in her hand.

Greg headed for the back door.

"No!" Rebecca's pulse started to race. "No dogs in the kitchen." Ever.

"He just sits right there inside the door," Greg said. "He always gets to come in and—"

"Absolutely not." Rebecca glared at him until he gave up.

"How do you know how much to make?" Serena asked. "I've never cooked breakfast for more than four before."

Rebecca wiped off her hand, then poured in some milk. "I worked my way through college cooking in a fraternity. The frat mom grew up on a ranch in Texas, so I learned country cooking." *Thank you, Maybelle.* She seasoned the eggs and then frowned. "Did I see cheese in the fridge?"

A second later, a block of cheese appeared on the counter. "Thank—" Her voice stuck in her throat as her eyes took in the hand holding the cheese. Dark tan, scars along the knuckles. Powerful and strong. She knew how easily those hands could pin a woman to the bed. Her stomach fluttered as if host to a wayward bird. "Thank you." Hauling in a bracing breath, she looked up.

His cheek creased, and his eyes crinkled. "You're welcome, sugar. It smells good."

Surely the heat in her face came from the oven.

Logan ran a finger down her cheek, moving closer until his chest brushed against her breasts. Her nipples tightened almost painfully as if they remembered his touch. As if they ached for more.

Bending down, he murmured, "Those pink cheeks, little rebel, make me wonder what you're thinking about."

Before she could think of anything to say, he tugged on a loose stand of hair and left the kitchen.

Chapter Five

"I won't take you home." Matt ran the razor across his chin, staring at himself in the steamed-up mirror in their cabin bathroom.

She'd finally run him to ground after breakfast, and now he didn't even look at her. Rebecca scowled and crossed her arms over her chest. "Matthew, I won't—"

"Sorry, babe," he interrupted. "But I've been looking forward to this vacation with the club for months. I'm not going to ruin it because you're too uptight to enjoy yourself."

"I'm not uptight," she said in a thin voice. "I just don't like strangers groping me. And I'm sorry. Coming here was a mistake."

"Not my mistake," he pointed out. He splashed water on his face to remove the shaving cream. "You can take the car if you want; I'll catch a ride with someone."

"I don't know how to drive a stick shift."

"Oh. I forgot. Well, then, I guess you're stuck until Wednesday." Turning, he said, "Logan's brother is taking some people to see the falls in Yosemite this afternoon. You said you wanted to see the place."

"I do." She clenched her hands so tight, her knuckles cracked. "Will you at least give me the cabin to myself? You can move in with one of the others."

"No." He patted his face dry. "We've found it works better if the men stay in the cabins, and the women wander around. Unless someone wants a free-for-all, and then we use the lodge room. So I need the cabin. But you're welcome to use it too. A couple of the women really enjoy threesomes."

Right. "That won't work for me, Matt."

He gave an exaggerated sigh. "Look, it's not my problem, but I'll talk with Logan and see if he has an empty cabin. I doubt it, but I'll ask."

"Thanks." *Don't overexert yourself.* She gave him a stiff nod and left. Matt might as well talk with Logan; if she asked for a cabin, she'd all too likely end up in his bed—again. She frowned. Last night hadn't been exactly her decision, and they hadn't done that much…really…but a second time would mean real sex. She pressed a hand over her stomach where her supposedly nonexistent libido turned a few somersaults. Damn.

Matt might be comfortable messing around with different lovers, but she wasn't. If she went to bed with Logan—as in making love—then it basically meant she considered her relationship with Matt over. She stopped and leaned against a tree, frowning. Could she ever get past seeing Matt with Ashley?

But they'd been so right together, and he'd said as much.

But would he be willing to quit the swinging club? *Doubtful, Rebecca, doubtful.* Where did that leave her? Breaking up and breaking the lease and being single. Alone.

Her breath shuddered through her, and then she tightened her lips. Life was what it was, and she had to face facts. A monogamous woman didn't belong with a man who wanted a variety pack of women. She sighed. What did that say about her inadequacies that he had to go messing around with other women? Sure, she could tell herself he just liked to swing, but that didn't help the underlying feeling that she didn't measure up. *Too big, too boring.*

With a sigh, she headed down the trail toward the lodge. Walking around a curve, she stopped dead. The dog stared at her from the center of the trail. *Oh God, oh God.* She took a step back, but it advanced on her. Its ears were back.

As it got within a foot, her heart pounded so violently, she thought she'd throw up. *Don't run.* Running made them jump on you and rip at you and...

It sniffed her jeans. She couldn't quite stifle the whimper, and it looked up at her, growling.

"Thor." Logan stood at the bend in the trail. "Come here."

Relief rushed through her and made her breath hitch. Yet she couldn't move.

Giving one last growl, the dog trotted back to its owner.

Logan reached Rebecca just as her legs crumpled. He caught her, his hands firm around her waist. "Easy there." He scooped her up in his arms, sat on a downed log at the trail's edge, and cradled her as easily as if she were a toddler. As his scent surrounded her, she managed to draw in a breath and then couldn't seem to get enough air.

Safe. She was safe.

Without speaking, he held her as she shuddered, as she burrowed closer into his arms, as her gasping slowed. After a while, she realized he was stroking her back, not fake reassuring pats, but long sweeps of his hand, warm and firm. Her breathing slowly changed to match the rhythm.

Finally, when she couldn't put it off any longer, she moved, trying to ignore the flush of humiliation. What an idiot she'd made of herself. Last night and now.

His arms loosened, and she sat up. "Thank you, Logan." She braced herself and looked him in the face, expecting pity. Maybe even some disgust.

His expression held only sympathy. And curiosity. "Thor is intimidating, I know, but I've never seen someone quite so frightened of him. Why?"

She slid off onto the log to sit beside him before spotting the dog standing a few feet away. She barely managed not to crawl back into Logan's lap. Why wouldn't it *leave?*

Callused fingers took her chin and tilted her face up, forcing her eyes from the dog. Thoughtfully, he studied her. "Why are you so scared of dogs?"

She did not want to remember any of it. Never. Forget talking about it. She tried to shake her head. God knew her voice wouldn't work right.

He didn't release her. His voice deepened. "Becca, answer me."

"One b-bit me."

"Keep going, sugar. I can tell there's more to it than that. When did it happen?"

"When I was ten." Under his level gaze, words spilled out of her, ugly memories she hadn't been able to share with anyone. "Skateboarding in the park and a dog..." The memory of the dog blanked her mind. Her hands fisted, and she jerked her gaze away.

"No, look at me."

When her eyes turned back to his, he stroked his warm hands up and down her arms.

"Tell me more. Was the dog big?"

She shuddered, remembering how it had come toward her, growling, teeth bared, the hair on its back up like the dog here. *The dog.* Where was Thor? She turned.

Logan cupped his hand around her chin. "Look at me, sugar. Big dog?"

She nodded and found her voice worked. Mostly. "Big." There were no words for the size of it. "It came at me, growling, and I tried to run away."

He winced.

"Yeah. The doctor said I shouldn't have run. But it was going to attack me anyway."

"Got it." He let go of her face and picked her up, setting her back on his lap. Without speaking, he held her against him. His arms around her were powerful, his chest solid. Nothing could get to her. She buried her head in his shoulder and sighed.

"Keep going. Get it all out," he said. "You ran. Then what?"

"It attacked, got hold of one of my legs. I fell." Her head had cracked against the concrete, and pain had been everywhere, striking over and over. "It... I would have died, except I screamed. A man had a baseball bat."

"God, sweetheart." Logan's arms tightened. "You were just a baby."

"They sewed me up as good as they could, but"—she shrugged—"I have scars." She could hear her classmates taunting, "*Ugly, ugly, ugly.*"

"Well, I'll take a closer look at them later," he said.

She stiffened. "You will not."

He chuckled and then lifted her like a doll, placing her on the log between his legs with her back against his chest. "Meantime, you and Thor need to make friends."

"No way." She tried to stand, and an iron arm locked around her waist.

"Give me your hand." He reached around her and put his palm in front of her waist. "Rebecca."

When he used that voice, that tone, why did she obey him? This wasn't like her at all, yet he made her feel so safe. Her hand crept into his.

His voice warmed. "Good girl." He shifted slightly. "Thor, get over here and say hi to the lady."

Thor paced over to them. When Rebecca tried to shrink back, Logan's unbending body behind her prevented it. Her free hand clasped his thigh, the fingers digging in as the dog came closer.

Its eyes looked mean, and she couldn't muffle a whimper.

Logan's hand held hers steady as the dog sniffed her fingers. "She's a friend, Thor. Stop picking on her; she's had a rough time."

As if it understood, the dog looked up. She was shaking uncontrollably, wanting only to run. It snuffled her hand again, and then it licked her palm.

"It wants to eat me," she whispered. "Please, please, let me go."

A laugh rumbled in her ear. "No, sweetheart. I'm the one that will eat you. Thor only licks people he likes. It's his version of a hug."

"Really?" She hadn't been this close to a dog since the attack. She'd cross the streets to avoid anything larger than a miniature poodle. If people had dogs, she didn't visit. "Look at his teeth." Sharp and huge and savage.

"Thor is a mixture, a mongrel. We figure he's part-shepherd, part-husky, and part-collie. Remember Lassie? Lassie was a collie." The matter-of-fact voice comforted her as Logan gripped her hand, forcing her to stroke Thor's head.

The dog's tail moved slightly, back and forth. Even Rebecca knew that was a good thing. Logan didn't let up, making her pet the dog over and over.

"Now huskies tend to be shy and don't really like people," Logan said, his voice a low murmur in her ear. "But shepherds are smart guys and want to hang out with humans, since they get bored easily. Collies are natural protectors. Anything that needs to be saved, a collie's your dog. All three breeds are accustomed to working with man."

Rebecca's muscles had relaxed, and after a second, she realized he'd released her hand. She was petting the dog by herself. And it let her. She pulled her hand back. Would Logan release her now?

The dog moved forward. Rebecca's breath caught, and she cringed back against the immovable body behind her.

Another paw moved forward, and then the dog laid its head on her knee and leaned heavily against her leg. Big, dark eyes looked up at her, and its demand couldn't have been more obvious if it talked. *Pet me some more.*

It—*he*—wasn't a monster. Her laugh caught on a sob, but she managed to lay her hand on his head and stroke his fur. *Soft fur.*

"Very good, sugar." Logan kissed the side of her neck. "You've made a friend, and Thor has someone else to nag into petting him. A good day's work."

He set her down on the log beside him before rising. Bending over, he placed a hard kiss on her lips, then snapped his fingers at the dog and continued down the trail. Rebecca watched them until they disappeared around a corner of the forest.

Well. She'd petted a dog, and he had wagged his tail and licked her. Her breathing and heart rate were still too fast, but she smiled. He liked her. *Thor* liked her.

She pushed to her feet and had to hold on to a tree until her knees stopped wobbling. Starting down the trail, she remembered something Logan had said. "*No, sweetheart. I'm the one that will eat you.*"

The flush started in her face and didn't stop until her toes curled in her sneakers.

* * *

Jake had returned, thank Christ, and Logan not only didn't have to play nice with the people but he'd even caught a two-hour nap. The swingers who had gone in the van with Jake to see Yosemite Valley had returned, pleased with their afternoon. The few swingers who remained at the lodge had been—occupied—and were also pleased with their day, sharing tales of their adventures over the supper table.

Happy campers made for return business.

With a grunt of satisfaction, Logan poured himself a glass of wine and wandered out to the lodge room. Taking a chair a small distance from the crowd, he settled in to enjoy the aftermath of a good meal.

Rebecca was quite a cook. This morning the breakfast she'd made had taken his breath away. And supper had been roast beef with potatoes stewed in the juices, gravy, more biscuits. Hell, he could live nicely on just those biscuits alone. She'd even baked a cake. From scratch. He hadn't had food like this since he'd left his parents' ranch in Oregon.

Leaning back in his chair, he sipped his wine and studied the little rebel. A drawing pad propped on her lap, she created caricatures of the others to much acclaim. He shook his head. For an artistic type, she sure had no sense of how to dress. After coming back from Jake's Yosemite tour, she had changed into another of her ugly shirts, the ones that covered up every curve she had. Idiot woman. Even one of his flannel shirts would show her figure off better. Didn't she realize that a man would never notice the roundness of her waist when she had so much roundness above it?

Maybe he should tell her that.

God, she'd felt good underneath him this morning, and on his lap later. He could have resisted her physical attraction—maybe—but when she'd trembled in his arms as he made her pet Thor, he'd lost the battle. That damned vulnerability brought out every protective instinct of a Dom.

Then there was that moment when Thor laid his head on her leg, and her delight replaced fear. He had hoped for a truce between her and the dog, and instead he'd gotten the beginnings of true love. He sipped his wine and sighed. He hadn't expected the city girl to be so sweet. Like desert sand, she kept shifting on him until he could never be certain of his footing.

One thing he'd decided... She'd be underneath him again before the end of the weekend.

With a smile, he turned far enough to put her fully in his sights. She was aware of his attention, flushing every time she met his gaze, and even from here, he could see her breathing turn fast and shallow. A timid little rabbit when it came to sex, but trap her he would, even against his better judgment.

Giving her a break, he leaned his head back against the chair and relaxed. He had a long day's work in front of him tomorrow, and hopefully he'd get some sleep tonight.

"...BDSM."

With that word, Logan's attention turned to the conversation going on, and he opened his eyes. What were they talking about?

"I thought swinging and bondage stuff were the same thing," Rebecca asked the couple on the couch across from her, setting her pencil down.

"No, swinging just means open sex. Now BDSM means"—Mel rubbed his ruddy face as he thought—"three different things. SM for sadomasochism. And BD is..."

"Bondage and discipline," Ginger said. "Tying people up and that sort of thing. And the DS part stands for domination and submission."

Not bad, Logan thought. They'd gotten the acronyms correct at least.

He noticed Jake had disappeared, so he rose to make the wine rounds. Part of their lodge host duties involved playing bartender. He enjoyed the chores most of the time, and before they became too annoying, the lodge would empty out, and he could enjoy the quiet.

He filled glasses as he went around the room, reaching Rebecca just as she asked Mel, "I knew about the S and M stuff, and I've heard of bondage. But the domination and submission? I don't get that."

The Dom in him couldn't pass over an opportunity like this, not from a woman he wanted. After setting down the wine bottle, he leaned over and threaded his fingers in her hair. When he tightened them, he had control.

She jumped in surprise and tried to wrench away.

With a steady pull on her hair, he forced her to look at him.

Her mouth opened.

"You do not have permission to speak," he growled.

Not only did she stay silent but her pupils dilated slightly. Her cheeks flushed.

The sands shifted under him again. *Spirited. Vulnerable. Sweet.* Could she really be submissive also?

Releasing her, he cupped her chin in his hand, seeing the stunned look in her eyes. "That's domination, pet," he said. He smiled slowly as her body quivered in his grasp, confirming his impression.

And that's submission.

His blue eyes seemed to pin her to the chair even as his hard hand kept her head from moving. His voice, his command, kept her silenced, and somehow, someway, her body not only let him but she was shaking inside as waves and waves of heat went through her. She stared up at him helplessly and knew if he wanted to take her, here and now, she'd let him.

He ran his finger over her lips, and she realized her mouth was open, her breathing fast. His cheek creased with his smile. And then he turned and left her sitting there in the chair, staring at him.

Chapter Six

"There are no empty cabins?" Rebecca set her hands on her hips. "Well, that's just great. What am I supposed to do?"

The after-dinner conversations had broken into increasingly hot displays. Matt sat on the couch with Ashley almost in his lap. She played with his hair, giving Rebecca a superior look.

"You could join in and have fun like the rest of us," Matt said. "How can you know you won't like it if you don't give it a try? I know Christopher and Brandon wanted you to join them, and so did Paul and Amy."

Ugh. "Not interested," she said crisply. "So…" God, what was she going to do?

"Logan suggested you talk to him, and maybe he could work something out," Matt added, then slid his hand into Ashley's low-cut blouse, his attention obviously not on the conversation.

Giving a huff of exasperation, Rebecca stalked out of the lodge. Screaming in fury might not help matters, but damn it all, hadn't she been in this same position yesterday? Sleeping on the porch swing meant risking hypothermia again, so that was out. Mouth tight, she headed down the trail. Matt used the cabin last night. Fairness dictated that she get it tonight—to herself. After all, that's why God gave locks to humankind, to keep out idiot males.

With the sun gone, the air temperature had dropped rapidly, and she shivered. In the stillness of the forest, the sounds from the lodge seemed distant as her sneakers crunched on the pine needles covering the trail. Almost there, she stopped. Heck, she'd left her art bag in the kitchen. She glanced back down the trail and shrugged. Not worth going back in the lodge again, not considering what would be going on.

At her cabin, she stepped onto the tiny porch, grabbed the doorknob, and...

Giggling came from inside the cabin. A man's laugh— Paul—and the bed started creaking in an unmistakable fashion.

Well, damn, damn, damn. She backed away rather than kicking the door like she wanted. So much for that plan. God, Matt must plan to have a foursome in there later. *Ew.*

She turned and went back down the trail, scuffing her feet, watching the dust glitter in the early moonlight.

She ran into a solid wall and let out a humiliating squeak.

Powerful hands gripped her arms, keeping her from falling, and she looked up into Logan's face.

"Jesus, just kill me and have it over with," she said, putting her hand on her chest where her heart was trying to pound its way out.

"Sorry, sugar."

"Sure you are," she muttered. He didn't sound sorry at all, more like he was trying not to laugh, the bastard. "I needed to talk to you anyway."

From behind Logan, Thor walked forward, an ominous-looking beast in the dim light on the trail. Rebecca stiffened, then sucked in a breath and held her hand out. *Don't bite me; don't bite me.*

Thor sniffed her hand, then, with his nose, nudged her hand up. *Pet me.*

With a choked laugh, she dropped to her knees and did just that. Furry and solid, the dog didn't want anything more from her than some affection. Within a minute, he sprawled over her knees, half in her lap, and Rebecca rubbed his chest and got an occasional tongue swiped on her chin.

"Are all dogs like this?" she asked Logan. A tiny bit of worry remained inside, and yet there was something incredibly comforting about having the big, warm body in her arms.

"Thor's one of a kind," he said. "He doesn't trust too many people, so consider yourself honored."

She buried her face in the soft, soft fur and sighed. "I like you too," she whispered into one furry ear and saw his tail move in response.

"Let's get back before you freeze." Logan offered her a hand. "Thor, out of the lap."

The dog moved, and Rebecca let Logan pull her to her feet.

He walked beside her toward the lodge, not releasing her hand. "No place to stay for the night, I hear."

"No." Annoyance at Matt made her voice sharp, and yet anticipation rose within her like champagne bubbles. Logan's big hand engulfed hers in warmth as they climbed the steps to the porch. "Do you have a storage shed or something I can use?"

The light from the lodge windows highlighted the hard planes of his face. "You are going up to my quarters and to my bed." He put a finger under her chin and lifted until her face was fully in the light. "You may say, 'Absolutely not,' right now."

He studied her face while her mind yammered in confusion. Her body had no qualms, and heat swept through her from stem to stern. His lips quirked. "That's what I thought," he said, as if she'd answered a question. "Come."

After opening the lodge door, he set a hand on her lower back, pushing her forward to the private door behind the desk. He tapped a code into the keypad and steered her inside and up the stairs to his rooms. Thor slipped in before Logan closed the door. "Shoes off, Becca," he said, removing his boots. Her sneakers looked tiny beside his.

As the dog curled up on a pile of blankets in the corner, Logan pointed to the couch. "Sit there, sugar." The leather couch sank under her weight, trapping her in softness. She glanced around, noting the TV had been concealed behind a lush tapestry. Logan definitely liked his comforts with the cushy chairs and couch, the deeply plush rug in front of the fireplace.

When classical baroque music drifted through the room, Rebecca blinked. This hard-faced mountain guy liked Bach?

After stirring the coals in the fireplace, he tossed on more kindling and a big log.

"Beer, scotch, screwdriver, or wine?" he asked.

"A screwdriver, please." The healthy orange juice surely compensated for unhealthy alcohol, right?

He crossed the room into the kitchen silently, like a large animal, and darned if she didn't feel like prey. She edged over to the corner of the couch. Pulling her legs up to her chest, she wrapped her arms around her knees and tried to watch the fire. Didn't work. Had she gone insane?

Of course, he was gorgeous, in a rather scary Vin Diesel sort of way. And she was a healthy female...who had just refused to go to bed with any number of willing men and instead let this man lead her up here. Not that he'd really asked. But her mind kept telling her she'd gone nuts.

"That's a very defensive position."

Her eyes jerked up to see him looming over her. Her stomach did that fluttery thing again, and she swallowed. "No, it's comfortable. I—"

"Rebecca," he interrupted. He set her drink down on the coffee table rather than handing it to her. Putting a finger under her chin, he tilted her head up. His eyes were gray in the bright lights, his jaw stern. "Try again, and give me the truth this time."

The quivering inside her increased, and her mouth went dry. But she raised her chin. "I... Yes. It's defensive. I'm rather nervous, okay?"

His smile was warm and approving, and why something so simple should make her feel good inside didn't make sense. Dammit, she'd always seen herself as strong. Confident. How did he have this effect on her?

Pulling her legs down with firm hands, he stripped her of her defensive position. She resisted long enough to get a sharp look, and then let him have his way. Damned if she knew why.

To her surprise, rather than setting her feet on the floor, he left her legs outstretched on the couch. Then he sat down on the edge of the couch next to her hips, leaving her no room to scoot away. Her corner had turned into a trap. A glint of amusement appeared in his eyes, and then he handed her the screwdriver.

She took a few hefty swallows to ease the dryness in her mouth.

"Enjoy it, since that's all the alcohol you get tonight."

"Why?"

"So you have a clear head."

She looked up to catch him regarding her thoughtfully.

"I'm going to show you more about dominance and submission tonight," he said.

"Excuse me?" she said slowly.

"Oh, you heard me." He ran a finger down her cheek. "And you're interested, although you don't think you should be."

Her mouth opened, but she couldn't deny it. She could feel her heart thudding loudly, loud enough she hoped he couldn't hear it. A brief hope, since he trailed his fingers down her neck to rest on her pulse there. His eyes crinkled.

She licked her lips. "So what does this"—saying the actual words would make them way too real—"stuff involve?"

"It's easy enough, little one." His fingers slipped open the buttons on her shirt until it gaped open. When she lifted her hands to close it, he growled, "Don't move."

She froze.

His smile warmed. "That's how it works, Rebecca. I tell you what to do, and you do it. Very basic."

"Wh-what if I don't want to do what you say?"

"Good question." His gaze on her face, his fingers trailed over the top of her bra, awaking nerves throughout her body. "If something I do is unbearable, either physically or mentally, you say, 'Red,' and everything stops. That's your safe word. Red."

Red. She repeated it in her mind and then frowned. "What if I say stop or no?"

His eyes didn't leave hers. Direct. Even. "Then I continue."

He stripped her shirt off as easily as if she were a baby, then the chemise she'd worn under it for extra coverage. A second later, her bra loosened, and he tossed it away. She covered herself with her hands.

He gave her a remorseless look. "No, I don't think so." Taking her wrists, he lifted her arms. "Put them behind your head." He moved her hands to the nape of her neck. "Lace your fingers together."

When she complied, he nodded approval. A very strange game, she thought. This is only a game. A game sounded...safe. But her breathing quickened. As if her skin sensitized in anticipation of his touch, she became aware of the smoothness of the leather behind her back, the warmth from the fire heating her right side, with coolness on her left.

She could feel her pussy grow wet.

Having her hands behind her head pushed her breasts forward. With a smile, Logan cupped them in his big hands. His thumbs rubbed over her nipples, sending zings of pleasure straight to her groin. "You know, my mother was built like you," he said. "Medium height and lush. In spite of having five kids underfoot, my father had trouble keeping his hands off her. I'm beginning to see why." His fingers rolled one nipple, and the pressure increased slowly until it felt as if there were an open channel of electricity between her breast and her pussy. Nothing had ever felt like that. She started to move, to bring her hands down, and his brows drew together. His face turned harsh. "Don't move, pet. There are consequences for disobedience."

Consequences? She opened her mouth, and he kissed her, his tongue plunging within, seizing possession. He caught her hair in his fist, holding her so he could kiss her thoroughly, so thoroughly that her toes were turning up inside her socks. Releasing her lips, he moved down slowly, his five o'clock shadow scratchy on her neck, his lips warm velvet. As his mouth got closer to her breasts, she realized she was holding her breath, needing him to touch her, kiss her there. He pressed a kiss between her breasts, nuzzling one side, then the other. Her breasts felt heavy and swollen.

His tongue flickered over one nipple. Hot and wet. A puffed breath cooled her skin, and the peak tightened, just before he took it into his mouth. A forceful sucking, then he pressed the nub against the roof of his mouth.

Her nipples engorged, throbbing with the beat of her pulse, sharp pulses of need shooting through her. Her mind seemed to shut down, her body taking over as the sensations continued. Almost frightened, she grabbed his shoulders.

His teeth closed on her nipple, delivered a sharp nip that sizzled straight to her core and made her jerk. "Put your hands back, little rebel," he growled.

She wanted to whimper. When she put her hands back and he secured her wrists with an inflexible grip, wetness seeped between her legs. A thrill sizzled through her when she realized he'd trapped her hands so he could do whatever he wanted. *God, this is so wrong.*

His mouth closed over her other breast, his tongue teasing her nipple. A nip fuzzed her brain, another arched her up to him. He laved the tiny hurt. Her breasts were so tight and swollen, they ached.

Releasing her, he sat back on his knees and stripped off his shirt. She couldn't take her eyes from his chest and the way his muscles flexed with each movement he made.

"Time to lose the rest," he said, undoing the button on her jeans.

She grabbed his hands. No way. Her breasts were all right, but her stomach and hips. And thighs? She looked up at the glowing amber glass on the ceiling fan, the lantern-style lights on the walls. Way too much illumination. Yes, he'd probably gotten a glimpse of scars and jiggles before, but no need to give him a nice, long look now. "Maybe we should move to a bed," she suggested. And get it on under the covers. Excellent idea.

As his gaze followed hers, his eyes narrowed. He cupped her cheek, watching her face, and his other hand slid her zipper down. She stiffened. Darn it, she didn't want him to see her like this. She glanced at the lanterns again.

Without a word, he rose and walked around the room, flipping off the lights. The crackling fire glowed golden on his bare shoulders as he returned to sit beside her.

Had she been that obvious? Surely he didn't know why she'd been nervous.

"We're going to have to deal with your self-image one of these days," he murmured, shattering that hope. He unwrapped her arms from her waist and replaced them behind her neck. "You don't trust me enough for me to cuff your hands behind your back, sugar. But you are sorely tempting me. Leave your hands there. Are we clear?"

Cuffs? Oh my God. "Clear. Yes." But the thought of being restrained like that sent quivers into her stomach. Was it nerves or excitement? She couldn't tell.

He smiled into her eyes. "Like that thought, do you?" Without a moment's hesitation, he yanked her jeans right off her. She felt exposed as he traced a finger over her breasts, down the pudgy stomach she tried to suck in. With the same finger, he hooked her panties and pulled them slowly off.

Here she was, naked, and he still had his pants on. Why did that bother her so much right now? She'd had lovers before, but something about the way he treated her kept her off balance.

Aroused.

He set his hand against her pussy, pressing lightly, as if he could feel the heavy throbbing. Leaning forward, his hand still between her legs, he kissed her lightly but pulled back when she tried to deepen it, giving her only what he wanted. With her hands behind her head, she couldn't pull him closer.

"If you were mine, this would be shaved. Bare to the world." Watching her face, he slid one finger through her wet folds, making her insides clench. "Bare to my touch."

Chapter Seven

Logan rose to his feet. "There are a few basic rules that most Doms and subs follow."

Rebecca sat up and pulled a loose blanket from the back of the couch over her lap. Her lips formed the word *Dom*. That must be short for dominant and then sub for submissive. This was a whole new world, wasn't it?

"While we are...we'll call it playing, you don't speak without permission. You will call me 'Sir,' and if given an order, your only response should be, 'yes, Sir.' You kneel on the floor unless given permission otherwise." He paused and tilted his head.

Rebecca frowned. This sounded an awful lot like slavery; she didn't like it at all. But her pussy had tightened, burning as his words continued. Still processing his words, she looked up. He'd crossed his arms, and his eyes almost froze her. "What?" she asked.

His brows drew together, and he pointed to the rug at his feet.

Oh spit. Don't talk. Say, yes, Sir. Kneel. *Kneel.* She slid off the couch onto her knees, put her hands in her lap, and tried to look properly repentant. Something inside her wanted to laugh.

"Better." Logan bent and with firm hands separated her knees to expose her crotch. "Some Doms want a sub's hands open like this"—he placed her hands on her thighs, palms up—"but I prefer your arms behind your back, fingers laced together." He tilted his head and waited until she complied.

At the feel of his hands on her legs, positioning her as if he had every right to do so, her laughter disappeared. Her body abruptly turned on as if he'd hit a light switch. One hundred watts' worth. With her hands behind her back, her chest arched forward, as if her breasts were—

His eyes on her face, he knelt in front of her and cupped her breast, lifting it slightly. Heat seared through her in a massive wave.

He smiled slowly. When his thumb circled the nipple, her insides turned to liquid. "Now your body is open and available for my use." His voice rumbled in her ears. He touched each breast, fondling her nipples until they ached. Then his hand slid between her legs as if he had every right to just touch her...

She felt his fingers stroke through her folds, one sliding inside her, and she inhaled sharply at the intimate touch. She lifted to escape the probing finger and received a stinging slap on her bare thigh. "Don't move, sub," he snapped, mouth firm in displeasure.

Something quivered inside her in pleasure and need.

Removing his hand, he stood in one lithe movement. When she looked up, he shook his head. "Keep your eyes lowered. When in the slave position, you don't look up."

Her mouth dropped open. *Slave?*

She heard him chuckle. "That's what the *position* is called. You're not a slave, little rebel; you're a sub. Usually slave means someone in a full-time submission and domination relationship; that's not something I do."

Whew.

His callused hands closed on her bare shoulders, easing the rigid muscles. "Relax, Becca. This is an exploration, not a life sentence." His hands were warm and knowledgeable, and her shoulders began to loosen. "And there's some exploration I have yet to do," he whispered in her ear.

From under her eyelashes, she watched as he walked over to a closet and took out a big bag and a black pillowlike thing the length of a couch cushion, only taller and wedge-shaped. He tossed the cushion on the floor in front of the fire, set the bag beside it, and crooked a finger at her.

She rose, striving for grace, pulling in her stomach. With a smile, he grasped her upper arms, pulling her onto her toes in a show of strength that made her stomach quiver, yet his kiss was gentle. Almost tender.

He scooped her into his arms and laid her on the wedge thing, only rather than using it as a back support, he put her head at the low end and her butt at the high one, her legs dangling off the edge. "Now, Becca, I'm going to buckle your legs down and give you a feel of restraints."

Her eyes widened. "But—"

"Silence." He grasped her ankle. "Only your legs. I'm leaving your hands and arms free." He smiled slightly. "You don't know me well enough to trust me completely. And rightly so." He pulled her leg out, down the side of the wedge, and wrapped a Velcro strap around her ankle, then did the other side. With her bottom on the tallest part of the wedge, and her legs parted widely, her pussy'd been put up for display.

She tugged at her legs. When she couldn't move them, as she realized how open she was, a tremor ran up and down her body, then more, unstoppable and unending.

"For this time here, little rebel, your body is mine to play with and to use." His hands curled around her thighs, pushed them farther apart. "Do you remember your safe word, the word you use to stop everything?"

"Red."

His firm hands massaged her thighs, his touch moving ever closer to where her clit throbbed. Bending forward, he blew on it, the warm air shocking. "Very pretty pussy you have, Becca." With a wicked smile, he ruffled her pubic hair and murmured, "A little red fox."

His thumbs spread her outer lips open, and cool air slithered against her inner labia, making her shiver. Gently, he massaged the outer lips before moving inward. "Nice and plump," he murmured; then his fingers slid over her inner labia. "Pinkish red with a hint of purple." As his fingers slid up and down over her drenched opening, her whole pussy started to burn with need. "A bit swollen, but you'll be a lot more swollen before I'm through."

His tongue followed his fingers. As he licked over her, the feeling was so intense, she squirmed uncontrollably. And then his thumbs pulled her more widely open as his tongue flickered up the swollen lips to…there.

Her clit ached and throbbed as he teased around it, each slide of his tongue along the nub making the ache inside deepen. One side, then the other. He raised his head and looked at her, his face shadowy in the firelight. "I'm going to get you so swollen that you'll throb." His fingers stroked through her folds. "Enough that your clit pokes out and hardens like a cock."

The sub's eyes widened, and her legs jerked. Did she want to run away or beg for more? Logan wondered. The intensity of her responses evidently scared her and delighted him. As a Dom, he wanted to take her further and further. As a man, he wanted to bury himself in her and pound her until they both came.

A master's responsibility to his sub came first. They had more to explore together before he let his cock rule. With a gentle finger, he slid the tiny clitoral hood up, exposing the glistening pink pearl it concealed. He touched his tongue to it, just the merest flicker, and felt her legs quivering. He worked his tongue over the fragile folds of the hood, up and over, then back down the other side.

Her breathing increased. He glanced up to see her knuckles whiten. That iron control of hers would get a beating now.

He inserted one finger into her, the hot, slick feeling incredibly tempting. He wanted to thrust himself in there so deeply, his balls would bounce on her ass. As he withdrew his finger, the walls of the vagina clenched around him, trying to hold him in.

He slid back in and out, added another finger. A moan broke from her. "Logan..."

He slapped her thigh as a stinging reminder. She jumped, and her soft mouth opened in surprise.

"Don't forget, little rebel, or I'll have to really punish you."

He felt the clench of her vagina, confirming his earlier impressions. Punishment turned her on. How much remained to be seen. He looked forward to finding out with an anticipation he hadn't felt in years.

As he slid his fingers in and out, the thigh brushing his cheek trembled uncontrollably. He pressed upward inside her until his fingertip found her G-spot, still rough and bumpy. His finger pulsed against it, and at the same time, he rubbed his tongue firmly against the side of her clit until it swelled, poking out from the hood.

Her moan urged him on. He'd never found anything as satisfying as pushing a woman past inhibitions and into pure passionate response. And this little sub had inhibitions and passion in equal proportions. Now her hips strained upward toward his mouth, but the tight restraints kept her immobile. Her breathing changed as her excitement soared in a true submissive's response to being vulnerable. To being controlled.

He eased his mouth back, rubbing his finger on her G-spot until it swelled and softened. Then he coordinated his attack to drive her further. G-spot and clit, finger and tongue, rousing the entire mass of nerves.

Her breathing turned to hard panting. Her whole body shook as she approached her climax. Her vagina billowed out around his fingertip and clamped down on his knuckles. Almost there. This was a dance with two partners. He might be in control, but her responses dictated his next move. And fuck but he loved her responses.

He slowed just to draw it out a bit and to enjoy the tiny whimpers mingling with her gasping breaths. Her vagina tightened further. Slowing even more, he held her at the brink as her body stiffened; even her breathing stilled.

Tempted to deny her, he paused, but that wasn't the lesson for today. Besides, he wanted to hear her come again. He sucked her clit into his mouth and teased it in gentle, pulsing pulls.

Her hips tilted up as her body arched, higher and higher, and then her vagina convulsed around his fingers in surging waves as she let out a long, satisfying wail. So satisfying he wanted to start over and do it all again.

But his cock might explode.

He released her clit reluctantly. She was incredibly sweet: heart, soul, and pussy. He couldn't believe she didn't have a husband and children running around her feet. Instead, she had him at her feet, and he enjoyed the hell out of it.

When he looked up, her nipples had tightened into tight buds of pink. As the rippling in her vagina slowed, he pressed firmly against her G-spot and licked over her nub, sending her over again.

And then again.

When he stopped to kiss her inner thigh, he could feel the glaze of sweat on her skin. Pulling out of her, he pressed a kiss just above her mound, smiling at the quiver of her stomach muscles under his lips.

"You're shaking, sugar." But not with cold. "Hands laced behind your head for now, please."

Face still flushed, her nipples just beginning to relax, she frowned at him.

God, she was cute. He frowned back and waited. Her arms lifted, reluctance in every tiny movement. And then her hands laced behind her head, arching her breasts up for his enjoyment and use.

He gave her an approving smile and unzipped his jeans.

As Logan stripped off his pants, Rebecca couldn't look away. The firelight flickered over his big-boned body, shadowing, then highlighting the contoured muscles. From a nest of dark hair, his erection stood out proudly, longer than she was used to and much thicker, not a slender sapling but a solid oak. His balls swayed slightly between his legs when he sheathed himself in a condom. Muscles flexed in his thighs as he knelt between her legs.

He lifted her heavy breasts with his hands. His fingers stroked the tender undersides, and a smile appeared on his face. He teased her nipples until they rose up, hard and pointed. "Does anyone ever get tired of playing with these?" he murmured.

His lips closed on a sensitive peak, and lightning raced through her body. He rolled the nub between his tongue and the roof of his mouth.

Her breath rasped at the slight pain. When he sucked forcefully, it sent a pulse of need straight to her core. Her hips moved, and her sex began to ache with the pressure.

He propped himself up on one forearm. "Time for one more toy. You may choose from a gag, wrist cuffs, or breast clamps."

She shook her head, not daring to speak.

"Oh yes." He ran his finger across her lips. "You're not here very long, sugar. Might as well give you a good grounding in the lifestyle. Choose."

She swallowed. She absolutely didn't want her hands restrained. To be gagged? No. "Clamps," she whispered.

"Good choice." He snagged his bag and pulled it closer, then removed a small box, taking out what looked like miniature clothespins. He held one up. Black rubber coated the ends. A tiny screw poked out of the hinge. "Since you're new, I'll forgo jewelry or weights. This time."

He leaned forward and sucked on one breast until the nipple jutted up. Then he attached the clamp, turning the screw until the clothespin pinched her nipple unbearably. She gritted her teeth, but he decreased the tension, leaving only an intense ache that somehow increased the throbbing in her pussy. He did the other one, and she stifled a whine.

Pain, and yet an unbearable arousal like she'd never felt before. God, she needed him inside her.

His hair, thick and tousled, fell over his forehead, touched his nape. His shoulders gleamed in the firelight, and she wanted to touch him so badly, her arms quivered with it. He smiled slightly. Gripping her forearms, he leaned forward on her, his weight and strength pressing her deeper into the wedge.

She couldn't move...anything. Her deep inhalation pressed her breasts against his chest, and the abrasion of his hair against her overly sensitive nipples made her hiss.

"We were discussing dominance and submission." His hands tightened on her arms, just to the edge of pain, and a thrill shook through her. "Your body is mine right now, under my control. Available for my pleasure." Propping himself up with one hand, he stroked down her body with the other, then pressed his palm firmly against her pussy and her throbbing clit.

She bit back a moan, unable to look away from his flinty eyes. "This is the most elementary of lessons, and the toughest one." One finger pressed into her, illustrating what he meant. He could do anything he wanted, and she could only lie there and shake.

He withdrew his finger. A second later, he slid the head of his cock through her wetness and then began to slowly push into her.

She was too tight, and her vagina tried to resist his size as his cock pressed farther. She panted, caught between the excruciating pleasure and pain. Her fingernails bit into his biceps as she tried not to panic. His eyes fixed on hers, he inexorably filled her until she felt as if she'd burst. When he finally stopped, deep inside her, she couldn't move. Her insides quaked around him with the shock of his intrusion.

She felt so vulnerable. So invaded, both by his cock and his intense eyes, which seemed to see right to her very heart.

Propping himself up with a forearm, he cradled her head. "Easy, little one," he murmured. "Take a breath." His thumb caressed her cheekbone.

His gentleness brought tears to her eyes, and she closed them so he wouldn't see.

He kissed her, his lips coaxing a response, velvety soft, until she opened and let him in farther. As his mouth moved warmly over hers, her body relaxed, bit by bit, the overwhelming fullness easing into pleasure.

"There we go." He nipped her lip; the tiny shock made her vagina clench. And that felt so good. His hand left her face to fondle her breast. When his finger rubbed over the nipple, jarring the clamp, pain then pleasure sizzled to the whole area he'd breached. "You feel so good, sweetheart, you're threatening my control."

His words helped. His callused hand grazed her breast, her side, her hip, nothing he hadn't done before, yet the act irrevocably changed by his presence within her and each sensation heightened to a consummate peak. "Look at me now," he said in a deep voice.

She lifted her heavy lids to meet his gaze. His face was shadowy in the firelight, his jaw tight. He moved within her, the feeling indescribable, shaking her foundations with intense pleasure. He eased out, and her insides drew together to fill the emptiness before he surged back in like the rush of the tide onto the beach, unstoppable. Her breath caught, and her grip tightened on him as if he could keep her from being swept away.

Watching her closely, he increased his pace, and her body stretched to accommodate him until each thrust brought only pleasure and the slow buildup of need.

He smiled, and the curve of his mouth changed his expression from dangerous to devastating. "Put your hands behind your head, sugar."

But... She blinked, realizing she'd grabbed him when he first entered her, and he hadn't made her stop.

His eyes crinkled. "You looked like you needed something to hold on to. But put them back now."

She did, lacing her fingers together, the position making her intensely aware of her vulnerable state and how he held all the power.

He rubbed his rough cheek against hers. "Next time your hands will be tied down," he whispered in her ear. "And maybe I'll tie your legs even farther apart and tease you until you scream."

Her vagina clamped around his cock, and he chuckled. "For now, keep your hands there. The next lapse, I will punish with something to redden that pretty ass of yours." His hand swept down and curled under one buttock, squeezing to illustrate his point.

She could feel the way her body responded, and she wanted to run away and hide. He talked about spanking her, and the thought made her wet.

"Ah, that confused look again." He nibbled on her lower lip. "We'll talk later. For now, your only thought is to keep your hands laced together. Is that clear?"

She nodded, tightening her fingers, winning a smile.

Then he moved, and she realized how very careful he'd been. Out and in, the driving rhythm sending shudders of need and shock through her body. Each thrust pressed him against her engorged clit, each touch reverberating through her until her vagina tightened around him and she began to wind tighter and tighter. As the pressure built, her hips tilted, trying to get more, trying to change his movements to hit her clit harder.

With a low laugh, he put his hand between them, sliding in the wetness there, then over and around her clit, keeping his touch firm. His fingers were so slick and—

"Don't move, sub," he growled, and she froze, her hands half out from under her head. She couldn't seem to move them back, though, as he touched her, over and over. His cock hammered her. He wouldn't let her move, and she whimpered uncontrollably as his fingers slid over her, and her insides coiled tighter and tighter.

Suddenly the room sheeted white, and she exploded around him. Spasms of intense pleasure shot from her core outward until even her fingers trembled.

He didn't stop. A husky groan broke from him as he increased the speed. A gentle pinch of her clit shocked overstimulated nerve endings. Her back arched up when another climax ripped through her.

As he pressed his forehead to hers, his hand slid under her to lift her hips even farther. He gave three forceful thrusts, then pressed deep, deeper inside her. His cock jerked against her womb slowly, then faster as his hand held them pressed tightly together. After a minute, he rubbed his cheek against hers.

When he raised his head, she held her breath. Now that he'd come, would he still look at her the same? Men changed sometimes, turned into different—

His fingers traced over the line between her eyebrows. "Now what's going through that head?" he murmured. "Hands down."

She brought her arms down. After stroking his hard biceps, she ran her hands up and over shoulders sheened with sweat. The way the smooth skin stretched over such powerful muscles mesmerized her. His scent wrapped around her, all male.

His lips moved over hers, giving her soft kisses. "Brave little sub. You did very well, and you should be proud. Hold on one minute longer." He pulled out of her and disappeared into the bathroom. When he returned, he released her from the leg restraints, then, with firm fingers, removed one breast clamp.

She slapped her hand over her breast at the unexpected pain as blood rolled back into it. "Ow!"

He chuckled. "They're worse coming off than going on." Ignoring her hand pushing him away, he undid the other one. With her lips pressed together, she almost managed to stifle the whine until he licked over one, teasing the nipple with a wet tongue.

Pain and pleasure. The whine escaped and turned into whimpers as he continued.

Lifting her up, he pulled her off the wedge and on top of him so they lay on the carpet in front of the fire. He was so tall, she felt tiny perched there. One hand pressed against her bottom, keeping her hips against him; the other threaded through her hair and pulled her down for another kiss.

No, he hadn't changed at all after having sex. She put her forearms down on his chest, propping herself up so she could look at him. Even with her on top, him on the bottom, the confidence still radiated off him. Seeing that absolutely masculine face and the controlled power in it, no one could ever doubt he was in charge.

Chapter Eight

Logan woke her twice more during the night, and in the morning, he took her again. He entered the walk-in shower, pushed her back against the wall, and lifted her up enough to slide into her. Not asking permission, just taking his pleasure when and how he wanted. She really shouldn't enjoy his behavior, Rebecca managed to think, before he leaned down to kiss her. Held in place by relentless hands, impaled by his thick cock... His actions and his control made her so hot, she came within a few thrusts, squirming and whimpering.

Afterward, he helped her wash, as if that too was his right. He knelt to soap her feet, then her ankles. As he ran the soap up her legs, she relaxed, her mind deliciously blank, until his fingers paused on her upper left calf. *Her scars.* She tried to jerk away, but he simply wrapped a big hand around her leg and turned her toward the light so he could see better.

"He got you good."

With her mouth clamped tightly shut, she couldn't manage anything but a nod. How had she been stupid enough to be naked with someone in a well-lit bathroom?

When he lifted her leg and kissed the scars, she gasped. He found the matching ones on the back of her right thigh, and she got another kiss. Rising, he said, "Seems like I felt something on your shoulder about here." His fingers traced the lumps on her right shoulder. Another kiss. Then he turned her around to face him.

She couldn't look at him. *Ugly, ugly, ugly.* Her hands fisted as the taunts of her fifth-grade classmates filled her head.

With a huffed laugh, he unclenched her hands and put them on his shoulders, then tilted her face up.

She kept her eyes averted.

"Look at me, sugar."

Warm water beat against her shoulders, the woodsy scent of his soap filled the air, and his patience was unrelenting. When she couldn't stand his silence any longer, she looked up.

His eyes crinkled. "There we go," he murmured. "You know, if you hate scars that much, we're going to have a problem. I have lots of them."

"But..." She huffed in exasperation. "You're a man. It's different."

His eyebrows rose. "You're sexist?"

"No. Of course not." She frowned as his meaning hit home. True, people viewed a scar differently on a man than a woman, but she shouldn't be letting the world get away with that. Really. "You have a point. I guess."

"Good girl." His deep voice was as much of a caress as the hand stroking her back. "Now, I kissed your scars..." He tilted his head in expectation.

At his unexpected response, she laughed. The last knot in her stomach unclenched as she started searching over his body. He did have a lot of scars. "How'd you get so many?" She traced her finger over a long slice along his side.

"Bar fight." He patted his chest. "Shrapnel." Left shoulder. "Bullet." He grinned at her horrified look. "I served in Iraq, Becca. I don't mind the scars. I got back alive and whole." Under his breath, he added, "Pretty much."

The war. She waited for him to say more. He didn't, and his face had hardened. Some hurts didn't show on the outside, she knew. Taking her time, she searched and found and kissed every single white mark and line.

When they finished washing, he made her come again with his soapy fingers and then insisted on washing away every trace of the soap, inside and out. God, if he hadn't held her up, her legs would have given out.

They still weren't all that steady a few minutes later as she knelt on the floor by her clothing. At least she'd managed to yank her jeans on, since she considered covering her big hips in the light of day a high priority. She secured her hair into a ponytail with a scrunchie from her jeans pocket and donned her bra and chemise.

Her brown top still looked clean. Nice and loose to hide her round stomach. She shrugged it on.

A snort of disgust came from behind her. "I don't think so." A second later, Logan pulled the shirt back off her.

"Hey." She turned and scowled, an ineffective response, considering how far she had to look up. "You can't—"

His low laugh stopped her, as did his finger tracing her lips. "You realize what a man thinks when a pretty woman kneels like that in front of him?" The crotch of his jeans was level with her face. So was the really thick erection bulging under the material.

Heat flushed her cheeks.

He chuckled and stroked her hair. "God, you're tempting, but I think you've had enough for one night, sugar." He tossed her shirt to one side. Dropping to one knee, he rubbed his knuckles against her chemise-covered bra and grinned when her nipples jutted out in response. "Can I talk you into wearing something of mine?"

She tried to tell her body to stop. The night had ended, and she'd come God knew how many times, yet just his touch made the burning start again. She shivered. *Concentrate, Rebecca.* "You're asking, not ordering?"

"I take command in sexual matters, little rebel. And only as long as you let me." His knuckles moved to her cheek, a gentle brush. "There has to be trust between a Dom and sub. And willingness. He can't take if she's not willing to give."

"Oh." Something eased inside her.

"But I'm very good at convincing people to do what I want." His grin flashed, causing flutters in her stomach. The way he looked when he smiled could cause pileups in the city. "Let me dress you for my pleasure today."

Yeah, when he looked like that, authoritative and laughing, she'd pretty much cave to whatever he wanted. "I guess so. With a few limitations. I won't wear something—"

"How about a flannel shirt?" he interrupted, chasing away her fears of purple negligees before they could take root.

"Ah, well." Flannel? Her? "Okay."

"Good." He studied her a minute. "Leave that lacy thing on."

"Flannel shirt, remember?"

"Silence, sub."

She sighed in relief when he returned with a long-sleeved shirt. The dark green matched the color of her eyes. He'd studied her that closely? A glow flamed to life in her stomach.

He pulled her to her feet and helped her into the shirt. "Oh yes," he muttered. His fingers tangled in her hair, and her scrunchie slid off, her ponytail falling into loose curls, waving over her shoulders.

"I—" Her protest died under a stern look.

Then he buttoned up the shirt as if she were a baby.

She looked down, and her eyes widened. He'd stopped at least three buttons short of the top, and when she moved, the gap in the front of the oversize shirt displayed not only her lacy chemise but a whole lot of cleavage too. Her mother would be appalled.

He ran his fingers over her collarbone and right down to the chemise, sending a rush of heat through her. "Maybe I should fasten more buttons," he murmured. "You're going to give me a hard-on every time I look at you."

Her hands fell back to her sides. With that incentive, damned if she'd button anything.

He grinned. "There's that dimple again. You like knowing you can make me suffer, don't you, sugar?"

"Darned right." She rolled the dangling sleeves up to her elbows. Flannel. Her mother would be horrified about more than the cleavage.

As she headed down the stairs a few minutes later, she felt as if she were returning to the real world after a night spent in a dream. Actually these whole few days felt like a dream. A strange world. Mountains and log cabins and woodstoves. Flannel shirts and cleavage.

And submission? Her face burned. What he'd done to her…made her do… What she'd enjoyed. *Oh God.*

Would she want this kind of kinky sex every time she went to bed with someone? Because her time with Logan was finite, ending on Wednesday. They both knew that. She was a city girl; he was a mountain guy. Refined versus rough. Very rough.

Especially his hands when he tied her ankles to that wedge thing. She leaned against the wall in the stairwell and concentrated on slowing her breathing. What if Matt had tried to dominate her? Would she have let him? Would her submission have heated up their sex life?

Get real. The thought of Matt with wrist cuffs in his hands made her giggle, and she gave up on thinking.

She had a grin on her face when she walked into the dining room and found Matt and no one else. Apparently indulging in an hour-long shower with Logan had made her late for breakfast. The hum in her body said it was worth every minute. "Morning," she said casually, walking past her boyfriend. Ex-boyfriend. Roommate. *Whatever.*

He turned and rested an arm over the back of his chair. "You slept in, didn't you?" His gaze slid down to her chest, and his eyes widened. "Ah. Yeah. So where did you spend the night?"

"Logan let me stay in his quarters," she said politely.

"Really?" His refined face twisted into an expression of concern. "You know, he's got a rather bad reputation, babe."

"What does that mean?"

"He's ex-military and has some problems, I hear. I prefer to have Jake as a guide; at least he won't go psycho on us."

"Oh, get real." Had she ever met a more self-assured man than Logan? Dangerous, maybe…but surely not unbalanced.

"I'm not joking. I heard he even attacked Jake once."

"Well, he didn't attack me." Not much anyway, unless that time in the shower counted. She could feel her nipples tighten. God, he really was dangerous if just thinking about him…his skilled hands…and his mouth, the way he could… She shook her head. Why couldn't she find a snowbank when she needed one? "He seems perfectly nice, Matt. You shouldn't listen to rumors."

"I don't think they're rumors, but whatever. So do you want to come with us today? Jake is taking us up to a waterfall where we can picnic. It's an easy hike, and there's a meadow filled with wildflowers, he says."

"Sounds pretty." And everyone will screw everyone in that meadow. "But I don't like group hikes. I'll just do my own thing."

Footsteps pattered across the main room, and then Ashley trotted into the dining room. She put her arms around Matt from behind, giving Rebecca a smirk.

Rebecca's palm itched to slap the gloating expression right off the blonde's face.

"Hi, babe." Oblivious, Matt patted Ashley's hand, before turning back to Rebecca. "Don't go out on a trail by yourself. That's one of Logan's rules, remember?"

She could feel her cheeks heat at the thought of Logan and his rules: " *You will call me Sir.*" "*Don't move, sub.*"

"Ah. Right. I remember," she said, giving Matt a sweet smile. Ignoring Ashley, she walked into the kitchen. As she poured herself a glass of orange juice, she shook her head. Truly she didn't want Matt anymore, but watching Ashley's hands on him twisted her stomach. Maybe because she didn't like the sly brat. Matt deserved better.

As if to prove Rebecca's opinion of her, Ashley said in a *whisper* loud enough to be heard in the kitchen, "Is she coming on our hike?"

"No, she doesn't want to come."

"That's good. You know, even before you said anything, I could tell from looking at her that she's, like, really frigid."

Humiliation twisted Rebecca's stomach. Pouring the rest of the juice in the sink, she set the glass in the dishwasher, resisting the urge to throw it at the cheerleader from hell. Or maybe at Matthew. How dare he talk about her?

She spotted her art bag still sitting at the end of a counter. She grabbed it, then walked out the back door, almost tripping over a dog.

Don't run. Breathe. Breathe. After three slow inhalations, she felt the panic subside, and she saw Thor, not a monster. "Hey, you."

His bushy tail swayed back and forth. Wasn't it odd how every time she met him, he had more personality? His mouth seemed to turn up into a smile when he was happy. His ears came forward when he was curious and went down when Logan scolded him. Even his tail had different positions like doggy sign language.

Feeling absurdly brave, she knelt beside him and ruffled the fur on his neck.

With a low whine, he shoved his head into her lap, knocking her onto her rear.

A breath of fear quaked through her, and then she laughed. "Bully." Sitting up, she wrapped an arm over his back. He licked her cheek and leaned in. God, he was sweet.

"So, my friend," she asked him and watched his ears prick up. "Shall we draw Ashley with a really big nose to match her tits? And plump her lips up to the size of dinner plates?"

* * *

Logan stood in the shadows of the forest, waiting for his brother and watching Thor cozy up to the city girl. He saw her stifle her fear—brave little sub—then laugh and hug the dog. She'd come a long way in just a day, hadn't she?

Damned if she didn't pull at him like a riptide off the coast. An assertive city girl whose vulnerability over her looks could break a man's heart. That stubborn courage that let her pet Thor. Her soft mouth and obstinate chin and willingness to share her passion even when he shocked her. The woman would never be boring, would she?

Jake walked out the back door and almost tripped over the two. Regaining his balance, he said a couple of words, making Becca smile. He walked across the clearing to join Logan, and they headed up Jackass Trail.

"Pretty little redhead there," Jake said casually.

"Uh-huh." Logan ducked under a low-hanging branch.

"Looks well used. Must have had a good night." A second's pause. "I noticed her wrists were bruised."

"Uh-huh." A low bark sounded behind them, and a few seconds later, Thor appeared on the trail, trotting to catch up.

"She's wearing your flannel shirt."

Logan knew that when an idea stuck in Jake's head, he held on more relentlessly than a damned bulldog. "You got a point to make here?"

Jake reached down to scratch Thor's head. "I thought we agreed not to fuck women in the swinger groups."

Logan stopped. Hell. They'd made that rule before opening the place, and neither of them had broken it. Until now. "She's no swinger. In fact, she almost froze to death on the porch to avoid becoming one. I put her in my bed then and..." Their father'd always said only weaklings use excuses. "*Stand up for what you did.*" Logan turned to face his brother and nodded. "Yes, I broke the rule."

"She's submissive?"

Logan sighed. They were both dominants, and Jake would see her appeal. "Yep."

Jake leaned a shoulder against an incense cedar, and a grin appeared on his face. "'Bout time. You going to keep her?"

"You're sure a nosy bastard." Logan scrubbed his face, feeling the stubble. He'd forgotten to shave again. "She's a city girl. She belongs there, not here."

"That's a shame. She looks good in the shirt—better than you do."

Logan grinned. She did look good.

"Why don't you keep her?" As Jake turned to scratch his back against the tree trunk, the dappled sunlight illumined his face. Hard and lean and tanned, like Logan's. But Logan's face lacked the long scar across his forehead, because he hadn't been attacked by his brother in the middle of the night and almost killed.

Logan forced his eyes away from Jake's scar, feeling the heavy weight of guilt in his gut where it never left. And neither would the memory of being trapped in a building, bullets ricocheting off the walls, fighting off a berserk insurgent. He'd awakened from the familiar dream that night with real blood covering his hands and a real knife at his feet. Across the bedroom, Jake had struggled to his feet, blood streaming down his face. "*Wake up, Logan, dammit.*"

Logan's voice came out harsh. "And when I have a nightmare and try to strangle little Becca, will she still be pretty then?" The lines around Jake's mouth deepened, and Logan turned away before he could see pity in his brother's eyes.

"You tell her about them?" Jake asked.

"That I have a tendency to try to kill people when I wake up on the wrong side of hell? Get real." Jesus, wouldn't that be a pleasant discussion? "I don't talk about my nightmares. Ever."

"You going to stay alone forever?"

"Damn right." God knew Wendy couldn't handle the stress. His wife had bailed out long before Logan had attacked Jake. "It doesn't matter anyway. Becca will go home on Wednesday, knowing more about herself. A win-win experience."

"Yeah? And what have you learned about yourself, bro?"

That being with a little rebel makes the loneliness worse. That guilt can't erase the desire for her soft body in his bed.

And that, no matter what, he wouldn't take the chance. "We have work to do," Logan answered and headed up the trail to where they had a fallen tree to move.

Chapter Nine

Jake left after they'd moved the heaviest sections of the tree. Logan found a shady spot and caught two hours of sleep before returning to the job of cleaning up the trail. He dragged the remainder of the debris off, shored up a section with rebar and wood braces, and cleaned out a dammed-up stream.

Wiping sweat from his brow, he scowled back down the trail. All that work, and only two miles or so accomplished. A flash of emerald green caught his eyes, and he frowned. Another flash. A hiker on the trail. One of the guests?

As he listened, he tossed more rocks into a muddy hole. Eventually he heard the soft crunch of dry pine needles. *Incoming.* He turned and saw Rebecca.

Pleasure shot through him at the sight of her, and he scowled in reaction. After leaving Jake, he'd decided to stay completely away from the city girl. She didn't need a damaged soldier, and he didn't need the heartbreak, because, dammit, she could easily break his heart. Another night of fun, and they'd both be hurting.

He glanced at the trail behind her and saw no one. "What are you doing hiking alone?"

A shaft of sunlight turned her eyes a clear green, and her hair glinted red and gold as she pushed back loose strands. "Everyone else went to some meadow, and I hate sitting around all day. I didn't realize you were up this trail. Sorry."

Ignoring his rules by hiking alone. Would have avoided him if she could. *Two strikes.* Anger stirred within him. Would she fail the third? He stepped closer.

Her eyes widened, and then he took her lips. She didn't pull away but offered her mouth, soft and open.

Threading his fingers through her hair, he tilted her head to give him complete access. When he stepped back, her face was flushed with arousal, and his anger disappeared under his own stirring lust. Dammit, she could tempt a priest to sin.

She broke the rules. Concentrate on that, not sex. He fisted the hand in her hair. "The rules of the lodge are no hiking alone. Did you forget?"

"Uh." She huffed out a breath. "No. I just wanted to hike and didn't have anyone to go with me."

Deliberate disobedience, but honest at least. He slid his hand down to cover her throat and grip her neck gently. "Rebecca. Don't do it again. Am I clear?"

"Clear," she said softly.

Under his fingers, her pulse increased, the compelling response of a submissive under control. He hardened. And changed his mind about escorting her back to the lodge, staying away from her, and not breaking any hearts, including his own.

"Since you're here, I guess I'll make use of you," he murmured.

"Okay, I'd be happy to help work on your trail," she said, her eyes on the shovel lying in the brush. When his fingers undid the first button of her flannel shirt, her startled gaze met his.

"I have a different kind of use in mind." He slid his hand under her bra and cupped her firmly. The startled intake of breath made him smile. He was thinking of all kinds of use.

* * *

The place where the swingers were headed couldn't be more beautiful than this, Rebecca thought, as they crested a hill and saw a tiny mountain meadow awash with purple and yellow wildflowers. The low hum of honeybees busy at harvest vied with the soft swish of the grasses in the breeze.

As they walked into the clearing, Logan released her hand and grasped her wrist.

Rebecca shivered, realizing with that move, he'd deliberately established she was under his control. She looked up and saw him waiting for her reaction. The man— the *Dom*—watched what she did more closely than anyone ever had. It made her feel vulnerable, almost as if he could read her mind.

As if she'd said just that, he stopped and tilted her chin up. "What was that thought?"

"Excuse me, but you don't get to know every thought I have." She tried to pull her face away, to back up.

He not only didn't release her but he crowded closer, his eyes darkening to a steely gray. "Normally during the day, your thoughts are your own. When you share my bed or when we are together like this"—he held up her arm where his fingers shackled her wrist—"then you will share your thoughts and your feelings. Openly and honestly."

She swallowed. The heat coursing through her body at his words contrasted with the quaking deep inside her. She liked talking with people but not sharing private emotions. They were meant to be private.

"Once again," he said softly. "You were thinking what?" His fingers kept her chin up; his thumb stroked over her cheek.

"I-I..." Like she'd tell him she felt vulnerable. Sure, and that would help everything feel better. "I was just..." *Tell him about the flowers and the—*

"Rebecca, do not lie to me," he warned, derailing that idea.

The sternness in his eyes and voice made her legs feel like overcooked spaghetti noodles.

His gaze softened. "Ah, sweetheart, this is very new to you." With a half laugh, he gathered her into his arms, his strong chest under her cheek, his arms like iron bands around her.

With a breath of relief, she put her arms around him. God, it felt good to be held. He scared her sometimes and—

"I'm waiting."

Dammit. Pulling back slightly, she leaned her forehead on his chest, staring downward. His scarred boots were firmly planted on the ground, and his jeans couldn't conceal the muscles in his thighs. This was a powerful man, and *man* was the operative word. Not a boy in an adult-sized body, but a man in the fullest sense of the meaning. Her defenses buckled. "I saw how you watch me so closely," she said to his boots. "Like you can read my mind."

"And how do you feel thinking I could read your mind?" Like a surgeon's knife, his words went right to the heart of the matter. When she tried to ease back, his hand curled around her nape, tightly enough that she knew he wouldn't let her move.

"Vulnerable, dammit. I feel vulnerable."

"There we go," he murmured, rubbing his cheek on the top of her head. His arms molded her against him. "Being turned on by that vulnerability makes it even worse, doesn't it?"

Oh God. Right there was the part she didn't want to think about. A quiver went through her, and he chuckled, damn him.

He led her to a tree stump, seated himself, and pulled her between his legs. "You're not a swinger, Rebecca." His hands tightened on her arms, holding her in place, and she felt herself dampen. "But you are a submissive."

The easy way he stated the fact made something constrict in the pit of her stomach.

Relaxing his grip, he ran his hands up and down her arms. "You had a taste of it last night, and you liked it. And now you're scared."

"Sure am," she muttered.

"You could run away, but that won't change your nature. It won't change what you want in bed."

That *so* was not what she wanted to hear.

"Since you're here...and I'm here, perhaps you should take advantage of the time and keep learning about BDSM."

An ache had started in her groin, set off by the feel of his hands on her. By the way he kept control of her body and the conversation and...everything.

However, he now emotionally, if not physically, backed off, waiting for her answer, giving her the choice.

If she wanted, she could enter this strange world. She shouldn't. Kinky sex just wasn't her, not at all. Then she remembered Ashley's hateful words, and her stomach twisted. *I'm really frigid.*

"Good to know."

She looked at him in horror. She'd said that out loud? "Matt told Ashley that," she muttered. God, how humiliating. But repeating Ashley's words and Matt's beliefs decided her. She'd come to Serenity looking for the answer to her sexuality, and she'd found a key in BDSM. Being ordered, being restrained... They turned her on, and yet she couldn't see doing this with just anyone. Any Dom.

She stared at Logan, seeing the strong jaw, the level eyes, his lips firm. He looked like a man who knew himself, one who didn't have any secret agenda to pursue. She trusted him. Mostly. He might scare her sometimes, but he wouldn't hurt her. He'd keep her safe.

Okay, then. If he wanted to open the door, she should take him up on it. She sucked in a deep breath, feeling as if she were jumping off a cliff. "I want to continue."

When his legs tightened, trapping her between them, and he started unbuttoning her shirt, her heart stuttered. "Do you remember your safe word?" he asked.

"Red, right?"

"Very good." The approval in his voice warmed her like a snuggly blanket and eased the tremors coursing through her. Her shirt flapped open, and he pushed it right off. Her bra followed, and she stood there half-naked. Outdoors. On a sunny day.

He caught her hands before she could cover herself and gave her an implacable look. "For the next hour or so, this body is mine to play with. Do you understand?"

A shudder ran through her when his hand caressed her breasts.

"Little sub, your answer is 'yes, Sir.'" He waited.

She tried to swallow, but all the spit was gone from her mouth. "Yes, Sir," she whispered.

"Very good." Rising, he moved her behind the stump to where the trunk lay propped up at an angle on the hillside. The exposed surface had been sanded smooth and black Velcro cuffs dangled from iron rings embedded in the sides. He settled her back on it and held out a hand. "Give me your wrists."

When she hesitated, he waited patiently, his eyes level. She trusted him, but nothing moved. An odd constriction around her chest kept her lungs from expanding as she stared at him. She really did trust him. She placed her hands into his.

His smile of approval helped, but then he lifted her hands over her head and leaned forward, putting his weight on her, anchoring her in place. Something suddenly tightened around one wrist, then the other.

She inhaled sharply and yanked. Her wrists were restrained. Tilting her head backward, she stared upward. Cuffs encircled her wrists, securing her to the tree.

She tugged, feeling on the edge of panic, her heart racing. "Logan? I don't like this." Her voice shook. She squirmed underneath him.

He took her face between his hands, halting her frantic movements, his hands unyielding but gentle. "Rebecca, look at me."

The command wrenched her attention back to him.

"I'm not going to hurt you, sweetheart. Do you believe me?"

She looked into his blue eyes. Stern, strong, powerful, but not cruel. He'd always told her the truth. She nodded.

A crease appeared in his cheek, although his lips didn't smile. "Good. The beginning of trust. I'm not going to leave you, and I'm not going to hurt you. Your job is simply trust. Trust me for—say, an hour—and afterward we'll talk about it. Can you do that?"

An hour? She'd be outdoors, chained to a tree, and half-naked for an hour? But his eyes stayed level, and her disquiet eased enough that she could give him a tiny nod.

His smile held approval. "Good girl." Bending his head, he licked over one nipple. She jerked as the hot sensation sizzled straight through her. Her arms tried to react, and she couldn't move, and that sent more heat washing through her. After a second, she realized Logan had stepped back, and his thoughtful gaze focused on her face.

When he cupped both her breasts in his hard hands, stroking the bunched nipples with his thumbs, she bit down on a moan. Her head thumped back against the tree as sensation after sensation rushed through her, and her next moan escaped.

"I'll take that as a yes," Logan murmured. He stepped back far enough to pull a strap over the little sub's waist, cinching it snugly over her bare stomach. It would both secure her more fully and take some of the strain off her arms.

She watched him with big eyes. Her breathing quickened, and he could feel the violent thudding of her heart when he palmed a breast. But her terror decreased each time her arousal grew.

He needed to keep reassuring her to retain her trust. But the edgy tension in her eyes and the shiver running through her were a Dom's dream. He walked a fine line, controlling himself as much as her, driving the scene for both their sakes.

He kissed her, taking her mouth slowly and thoroughly, letting his hands wander over her lush breasts. The nipples were peaked but still a pale pink, like cotton candy, and so velvety soft. He pleased himself for a while, licking and sucking until they spiked hard and pointed and turned a vibrant red. The curvy body under his hands slowly turned hotter than the sun on his shoulders.

She stiffened when he yanked her jeans and panties off, leaving her naked. To be fair and somewhat considerate, he stripped his shirt off.

Her eyes lingered on his chest, and she smiled at him. When her body eased slightly, he realized she believed he'd finished and the rest was going to be straight sex. Poor little sub.

He knelt, grasped her ankle, and enjoyed how she tried to keep her legs together in a silent protest. A Velcro cuff chained to an iron stake in the ground went around her ankle. He tightened the chain until her leg angled outward. When he did the same to her other leg, he heard a whimper of fear. Standing back, he nodded. Nicely exposed, her pussy waited for his touch.

Leaning forward, he ran his hands up and down her restrained arms until her breathing eased, and she stopped pulling at the restraints. "I like seeing you like this, little rebel," he said, capturing her eyes. "You are open to me in every way."

She couldn't conceal the quivering of her body at his words or the way her pupils dilated.

He took his seat on the stump. He and Jake had designed this piece of "equipment" carefully. The downed trunk made an admirable incline table and the sanded-off stump a convenient stool. A bondage group that weekend had provided test subjects so the cuffs and chains positioned a sub's pussy at just the right place for someone sitting on the tree stump.

His cock hardened as he looked at the little sub lain out like a feast in front of him. Arms over her head, her breasts jiggling slightly with her rapid breathing, the nipples in tight points of arousal. Glistening wet, her red-gold pubic hair glowed in the sunlight, and with her legs so widely spread, her labia peeked out, begging to be touched.

He ran a finger through her folds and smiled. She might be a tad scared, but she was also very, very wet. He slicked her pussy with her moisture and stroked over her clit, enjoying her high whine.

So the swingers thought her cold, did they? *Idiots.* Pausing for a second, he glanced across the tiny valley to Crone Mountain, where Jake had taken the others. Gold Dust Falls lay about…there, as a bird flies, well within shouting— or screaming—distance. He didn't give a damn what the swingers thought, but it obviously mattered to Becca. *Well, then.*

Uneasy with his silence, she squirmed in anticipation, and he leaned back to enjoy the sight. A soft, round submissive restrained. Squirming. Wet. He intended to use her well.

But first, she needed to sing. He leaned forward and slid a finger over one side of the engorged nub. He ignored her gasp of pleasure and ruthlessly and quickly drove her right to the edge of a climax.

When he lifted his hand, her hips tried to follow. Her eyes opened, swirling with need and then frustration when he didn't respond.

He simply watched her stew, giving her an indisputable lesson in who held the reins. Soon the tiny muscles around her mouth showed the anger overcoming her need.

He leaned forward and licked right over her clit.

Chapter Ten

Rebecca's head thumped back against the tree trunk at the feel of Logan's hot, wet tongue right on her pussy. A moan escaped. She tried to lift her hips, but the restraints were too tight, and she quivered inside from the knowledge. *Open for his use.*

As he licked her, each touch of his tongue shoved her back into need until her legs shook uncontrollably. *Oh God, please, just a tiny bit more. Don't stop.* His tongue teased her, increasing the intense burn.

Her body tightened as her climax approached, and her hips pushed forward as far as the strap allowed.

He stopped again.

No. Her clit felt so tight and swollen, it throbbed with every beat of her pulse. And she couldn't hold back a whimper. "Pleeeese."

He didn't answer.

She lifted her head to look down at him.

He sat between her legs, the sun gleaming off his tanned shoulders. When he met her gaze, the corners of his eyes crinkled. He set one callused hand on her thigh and squeezed.

The sensation shot straight to her clit, making it worse. Everything he did made it worse, but he deliberately wasn't letting her come. Damn him! She let her head fall back onto the tree. She yanked at her restraints, wanting to be free, to get away from him. "I don't want to play this game anymo—"

Something circled her opening, then plunged into her, fast and hard. His finger.

Her nerves inside shot awake like an electric current. "Aaah!" Her loud voice startled her, and she tightened her lips. *Outside. Don't make noise.*

He set his mouth on her, licking mercilessly along one side of her clit. When his tongue lifted, his long finger thrust in and out of her vagina, scraping against her inner labia. Another lick just at the edge, another glide of his finger through her swollen tissues.

Not enough. Never enough, and yet too much to let her arousal die. His finger and tongue worked her until she quivered at the precipice. Each exquisitely calculated touch strummed through her body, building sensation upon sensation until she couldn't think, could only tremble and strain for what seemed like forever. For that one final...

His mouth came down on her, pressing her clit between firm lips, his tongue swirling on top, even as he thrust two fingers into her.

The explosion of sheer pleasure crashed through her, and the blue sky seemed to splinter into bright white pieces. Her hips bucked futilely against the strap as wave after wave of ecstasy rippled from her center outward.

When he lifted his head and removed his fingers from inside her, her muscles went limp as if a balloon had been popped. She could hear high shrieking echoes rolling through the mountains. *Oh God. Had she—*

Before the echoes had died completely, Logan leaned forward, his lips closing on her clit. And this time he sucked gently and thrust two fingers into her.

Everything inside her contracted and then exploded again. She let out a long wailing cry as her insides spasmed around his moving fingers, as sensations rebounded through her with every tightening of his lips.

He drew it out until she was too exhausted to even moan.

Rising, he leaned against her, sandwiching her between his body and the tree trunk. Comforting her with his nearness.

She sighed and blinked at him. "I've never... That... Amazing." Her voice didn't sound right, too husky. Her throat felt raw.

He propped his arms over her raised ones and took her mouth, silencing her. His lips tasted of her as he kissed her, slowly, tenderly.

Gratitude filled Rebecca at his gentleness. Despite the lethargy of her body, her feelings roiled like a storm inside her. Her world had changed in the last two days and even more just now. Who had she become? But when he kissed her, she knew she was Rebecca, who was experimenting with BDSM stuff, not someone she didn't know at all.

When he lifted his head, he cupped her cheek with a warm hand. "You are wonderful, little rebel," he whispered. "Responsive and passionate. I have never enjoyed a woman so much."

His words thrilled her. Passionate? Her? Then she frowned. "You didn't... How could you have enjoyed yourself?"

"Sweetheart, I like to take control as much as you are aroused by giving it." He bit her shoulder, a sharp nip that sent a shock through her body. "To make you quiver, moan..." He gave her a wicked grin. "And scream."

"Oh." If she hadn't been held up by chains and the strap, she'd have been in a puddle at his feet. "Are you going to let me go now?"

The gleam growing in his eyes worried her. "No, little sub. Now I'm going to take you." He held her eyes, and she could hear the zipper of his jeans and the crinkling sound of a condom wrapper. His warm hands stroked up her thighs and spread her folds. He eased a finger inside.

She gasped at the intimate touch, the slide over her oversensitive tissues.

"You're wet. You're spread open for me. I'm going to fuck you hard, Becca, and all you can do is take it."

She could feel her insides clench at his words, and from the satisfied smile on his face, so could he. His finger slid out, and then his cock pressed against her core, sliding in her wetness, each graze of his hand across her clit making her jump. She looked down, trying to see.

"Keep your eyes on mine, Rebecca." His voice was deep, his eyes piercing. And then he drove into her, farther and farther, his thickness pushing her open, filling her to discomfort. Her breathing turned ragged. A thrumming started in her head as his groin made contact with her overstimulated clit.

He eased out. The next surge back in made her gasp.

With a faint smile, he increased his speed, each thrust forceful enough to tighten the ropes on her ankles and press her against the tree trunk. He moved a hand down to fondle her breast. When he squeezed her nipple, pain and then disconcerting pleasure seared down toward her clit to be met by the sensations expanding outward from the rhythmic, intense pounding.

And suddenly, the erotic sensations turned into feverish need. Now with each thrust of his cock, his pelvis dragged over her clit, making her whole lower half burn with urgency. Her hips swiveled, trying to rub her pussy against him.

He chuckled. "All right. I think you've had enough frustration for one afternoon." He reached down, and then knowing fingers stroked through her folds, rubbing to match the rhythm of his thrusts until everything in her surged with his movements, higher and higher. Her inside muscles clenched around him as he brought her to the peak.

"Come for me, Rebecca." The command hit her ears as his fingers pinched her clit, and he plunged his cock deeply into her.

Pleasure exploded outward like fire, shooting from her core to her toes and her fingers, until her whole body shuddered. Her pelvis thrashed against his fingers.

With a deep laugh, he grasped her hips with ruthless hands and hammered into her, hard and fast. And then with a low growl, he pressed in so deep and far, she could feel the jerking of his release against her womb.

With a quiet sigh, he leaned back far enough to release her wrists, then remained on top of her. She wrapped her arms around him, feeling the bunching of his muscles as he took some of his weight by resting his forearms over her head. His chest was hot and damp against her breasts, his face scratchy as he nuzzled her face and neck. When he lifted his head and took her lips, she opened to him, willing to give him whatever he wanted.

What a scary thought. She'd never felt anything like this before. She'd never been so out of control. Out of control? Heck, she'd never gotten a chance to have any control even from the beginning; he'd done what he wanted all the way through. That thought sent a tremor through her, making her clench around him again.

He felt it and lifted his head. "You going to tell me what that thought was?"

"No." She closed her eyes, wishing she could hide her face. What kind of person reveled in having someone else control them? The feeling of him looking at her was like warm sunlight, and his silence made her nervous. She sneaked a look.

His eyes were the blue of a winter sky as he laid his hand over her neck, just enough to let her feel his strength and the heat, and then he said in a rough, dark voice, "Next time, I'll tie you more open, so I can see all of your pussy."

Her insides spasmed.

"I'll turn you over and hold you in place while I take you from behind." His grip tightened infinitesimally.

Her vagina clamped down on his cock so hard, she moaned.

His eyes crinkled as he pressed a hard kiss to her lips. "You didn't need to answer me about your thoughts, pet. Your body gave it away."

She could feel the flush heat her neck and her face as he chuckled.

* * *

They made it back to the lodge in the late afternoon. Logan unlocked the door to the stairway and nodded toward his quarters. "Go shower in my quarters; I'll use Jake's. It won't be long before your group returns."

His little rebel wrinkled her nose at him, obviously not thrilled about eating with the swingers. When she got halfway up, he said, "Grab another flannel shirt from my closet."

A soft laugh was his only answer. He watched her take the last few stairs, enjoying the view of her round ass in tight jeans. He hadn't taken her from behind yet, and his statement from the afternoon had embedded the vision in his mind. Sinking his fingers into her soft hips and pulling her back onto...

Logan frowned up the stairs. Right now, she'd disappeared into his rooms; soon she'd disappear for good. And he'd miss her. He already knew that.

This afternoon, after he'd released her from the restraints, they'd worked together on the trail. She had wanted to help, even though she'd obviously never done outdoor work in her life. She'd stop every now and again to really look at the forest, spotting the tiny shrew scrambling back under a log, the doe and fawn watching silently from some brush, the hummingbird hovering over the flowering red paintbrush. He'd heard her mutter more than once, "*I need my paints.*" She laughed easily and worked cheerfully, uncaring of her hands or clothing.

She'd disagreed over where rocks should go in a stream crossing and argued with him. Hands on her hips, face pink, and eyes sparkling. He'd turned as hard as the rocks they were discussing. She'd won the argument too.

Logan grinned, then sobered and rubbed his face. The rebel had ambushed him with her laughter and intelligence. With those green eyes full of wonder. And with her surrender to him.

She was submissive in bed and feisty the rest of the time, not a slave who wanted to be under command twenty-four hours a day. After watching Jake and Mimi's failed relationship, Logan knew he couldn't tolerate that depth of submission. His gut twisted as he remembered Mimi's despair when Jake had uncollared her, and Jake's horror when he told Logan how she'd taken her life.

He heard the shower come on upstairs and shook his head. Why was he bothering to think about Jake and

Mimi…or Becca either? The woman would be gone day after tomorrow.

Fuck.

* * *

Rebecca arrived downstairs in time to see Logan disappear into a room she hadn't seen yet. She followed, and her mouth dropped open. A deluxe pool table on one side and a long rack of cues hanging on the wall. A Ping-Pong table and a foosball table occupied the middle of the room. A dartboard hung on the opposite wall. "Wow. Is this where you spend your winters?"

Logan turned, a smile lighting his eyes to a true blue. "Actually, we close the place down after the first snow and take off for warmer climes. Scuba diving, sailing, deep-sea fishing."

Oh, she could see him, cutoff shorts, barefoot. Shirtless. Especially shirtless, with that muscled chest and broad shoulders and dark tan. She shook her head—*bad Rebecca*—and said lightly, "Sounds like fun."

"It is." He nodded at the room in general. "Choose your game, rebel."

Hands behind her back, she strolled across the room like a supervisor. Everything was top quality; obviously the boys liked their toys. When she reached him, she grinned. While working in a fraternity, she'd learned more than just how to cook. "Let's start with pool. The winner gets to pick the next game."

He glanced down, and a crease appeared in his cheek.

She followed his gaze. Oh heck, hands behind the back while wearing an oversize flannel shirt was not a good idea.

"And the loser?" His eyes glinted in a way she didn't trust, especially when his finger trailed down between her breasts.

"Ah. The loser won't get to pick a game?" she said weakly. How could he turn her on like this, just with a touch?

He chuckled and handed her a pool cue. "Break."

Half an hour later, if she could have removed the flannel shirt without being indecent, she would have. The room felt way too warm, or maybe she was going through early menopause and having hot flashes.

How could Logan turn a simple game of pool into something erotic? All his attention appeared to be on the table, but his choice of shots always brought him next to her, and he touched her every time he walked past. A pat on her shoulder, a hand on her waist, a squeeze of her bottom. When she had to stretch out to make a shot, he'd stand at the other end, and his gaze down her front would be so heated that he might as well have taken her breasts in his hands.

He won by one stinking ball. Next time she'd try that sneaky way of distracting an opponent on him.

After putting their sticks away, he said, "The winner gets a victory kiss." He yanked her into his arms without waiting for her answer. With a fist in her hair, he tipped her head back and took her mouth. His other hand curved under her bottom and pulled her onto her tiptoes and against a rock-hard erection. Plunging his tongue deep, he possessed her in the same way he'd taken her body earlier.

All the teasing he'd done during the game was like kindling that now shot up into flames. She wrapped her arms around him and gave him anything he wanted.

With a low growl, he released her and then had to grab her arms when her knees buckled. He had a devastating grin, one that made her emotions turn all squashy. God, she could so easily fall in—She froze, her mouth dropping open. *No. No. Absolutely not.* No getting hung up emotionally on this man, no matter how gorgeous. No matter how he made her feel. Yes, he was smart and protective and…God, so male. He could laugh at himself and didn't get all territorial. When she argued with him about the trail, he'd just studied her solution and said, "*You're right. Your way is better.*"

The sex was great, and…he liked her.

Unnerved, she ran her fingers through her hair. But she lived in San Francisco. *I need to go home right now.*

"Becca?" He frowned down into her face. His hands curved around her upper arms, pulling her onto tiptoes. He took her mouth so gently that this kiss was even more devastating than the last. Encased in her chest where it should have been safe, her heart melted like wax in a hot sun.

"That looked like fun," a dry voice said from the doorway.

Rebecca spun. Leaning against the door frame, Logan's brother had his arms crossed over his chest. His blue eyes, a shade lighter than Logan's, danced with laughter, although no smile graced his lips.

"The horde is back, then." Logan pulled Rebecca to his side with an unyielding arm around her waist. "You're running late."

"It was a slow hike down after Brandon pulled a muscle, so it'll be a while till supper." Jake finally grinned. "I wanted to see if you were interested in a beer and a game of poker before we eat."

"Usual stakes?"

"Chores?" Jake snorted and then glanced at Rebecca. "Sure."

Well, while they were playing, she'd be able to cool down, give herself a good talking-to, and then maybe see about helping with supper. But when she tried to move away, Logan's arm tightened.

She looked up with a frown.

He ran a finger down her cheek. "How well do you know poker?"

"Not that well."

"Good."

* * *

Rebecca owed Logan a blowjob? All Jake had lost were two days of doing the dishes. Still a bit stunned and trying not to think about taking Logan's cock into her mouth, licking it, sucking... Darn it. She grabbed a Yosemite flyer someone had left on the dining room table and used it to fan herself.

When she stepped into the kitchen, she realized she'd arrived too late to do anything except make gravy for the mashed potatoes. Once finished with that, she noticed Thor sitting patiently just inside the kitchen door. The tidbits she dropped in front of him were woofed up quickly, and she couldn't help but notice his big teeth.

Shoving down her fear, she knelt to give him a hug, getting a quick lick in turn. His friendship was the best thing that had happened all week—except for Logan. *God.* She set her hand on her fluttering stomach. *Do not think about Logan.*

A pair of boots stopped beside her, and she looked up with a quick intake of breath…and let it out. Jake, not Logan.

Jake tossed Thor a piece of roast beef. The dog caught the morsel with an unsettling snap of sharp teeth that didn't bother Rebecca at all. *Much.*

"What a moocher." She scrambled to her feet.

"When it comes to food, he has no dignity whatsoever." Jake had a laugh even deeper than Logan's but less rough. "The minute food's on, he's in the kitchen waiting. He's never missed a meal since Logan found him." He grinned and ruffled the thick fur. "A homeless guy never passes up a handout, right, buddy?"

Thor whuffed and looked hopefully at the dishes being carried out to the dining room.

"Logan found him?" Rebecca prompted, trying not to look nosy.

"All skin and bones, trying to get into the garbage behind our hotel in San Francisco. He growled at me, and I would have left, but Logan—" Jake shook his head. "If something's wrong, he's just got to try and fix it. He sat out there for an hour, discussing the weather with Thor. And when we came back here, we had us a flea-ridden, scrawny dog." His words sounded harsh, but the hand stroking Thor's head was as gentle as...as Logan's.

She could just see Logan in some alley, sitting on a crate, long legs outstretched. Taming Thor's fear the same way he'd tamed hers. And when he snapped his fingers, Thor would have followed without a second thought. She bit her lip, feeling sadness curl up inside her. Logan wouldn't be snapping his fingers and taking her home.

As Jake walked away, Rebecca bent over and gave Thor another hug. "You're a lucky guy," she whispered in the furry ear.

"Rebecca, does anything else go out?" Paul yelled from inside the dining room.

"I'm bringing the gravy. That's all that's left." She planted a kiss on top of Thor's head, then poured the gravy into a bowl and followed the servers out.

She took an empty seat near the center of the table. To her amazement, Thor sauntered into the room and thumped down at her feet instead of choosing one of the brothers. She felt like a schoolgirl who'd received a star on her paper. Making a new friend: A+.

While stroking the big head leaning on her leg, she glanced at the club members. Sunburned faces, cheerful expressions. Sex made for hungry people. She knew that for a fact. Rebecca smothered a grin and helped herself to some potatoes.

A minute later, Greg rose to look over the food. His face fell. "No rolls or biscuits?"

"Get real," said Brandy, who had helped cook. "The only way I make rolls is if they come in a tube."

The grumbling from club members warmed Rebecca's insides. So maybe her thighs looked like grated Jell-O; she still cooked like a Texas version of Julia Child. *Thank you, frat mom.*

Making the rounds with a wine bottle, Logan set his hand on her shoulder to fill her glass, his touch causing shivers to run through her body. He whispered in her ear, "How can I bribe you to make biscuits for breakfast?"

Her first thought was so depraved that she could feel herself flush. *Oh God.*

He chuckled and rubbed his knuckles over her cheek. "You will explain that thought to me later. In detail." To her relief and disappointment, he moved on down the table.

If people hadn't surrounded her, Rebecca would have covered her face and groaned. The room had not only heated up, but even worse, her panties were wet, just from his brief touch. With a shaky hand, she picked up her wine and took a hefty drink. Not strong enough. Scotch would have been better. Jeez.

As she set her glass down, her gaze met Jake's. He raised an eyebrow, and his lips quirked in amusement before he resumed pouring wine.

She flushed again.

She cooled off slowly. Having Logan sitting at the far end of the table helped. If she concentrated on the conversations around her, she could avoid looking at him. The swingers had apparently had a fun day up in the meadow, thankfully on a different mountain than the one she and Logan had been on. The dynamics of the group had shifted again, she noticed. Ashley now sat between Brandon and Christopher, ignoring Matt. Brandy flirted with Paul and Amy. Rebecca choked at their discussion of the afternoon's sexual antics. Two men and three women in the water? An even bigger group in the meadow? Man, what... energetic...people.

Christopher waggled his wineglass. "What I want to know is who did all that screaming. Damn, it sounded intense."

"Oh, I know." Amy fanned herself. "If I'd have figured out where, I'd have gone to join in."

A chorus of agreement came from the others at the table.

Christopher frowned. "I thought it was you guys. She wasn't with us."

Frowns appeared around the table. Paul asked, "None of our women had a screaming orgasm this afternoon?"

"Not like that, more's the pity," Ashley said with a short laugh.

Oh, this wasn't good. Reaching for her wineglass, Rebecca contrived to glance down the table at Logan. He had an elbow on the table, chin in his hand, and his fingers covering his lips. He met her gaze, and amusement glinted in his eyes. And satisfaction. Satisfaction? Had he done that to her on purpose?

She would have to kill him. That's all. He must die.

She leaned back casually and took a sip of wine. And choked as a barrage of eyes turned toward her. From the heat of her face, she'd turned the color of a ripe tomato.

Matt stared, his mouth open so far, she could see his molars. "You? You were screaming like that?"

"Jesus, Matt. I thought you said she was a cold fish." Christopher eyed her speculatively, and she didn't like the gleam in his eyes. Or the way every man at the table started to look at her, like she'd suddenly turned interesting.

"Well, now, this is a surprise," Mel murmured.

"What I want to know is who she was with," Ashley said in a sharp voice. A moment later, she turned her cornflower blue eyes straight toward Logan.

Jealousy stabbed through Rebecca, a knife sharp enough to penetrate the sternum, and then heaviness settled in her stomach. Every woman in the place would scramble after Logan now, all of them better looking, all skinnier. She'd need to find a place to sleep again. She set her hands in her lap and squeezed until the burning in her eyes disappeared, and she could look at people with her chin held high. *Don't be an idiot.* They didn't have any relationship, after all. Her vacation ended Wednesday, and he hadn't wanted her for more than just a weekend slap and tickle, as it were.

He'd taught her a few things about herself, and she could only be grateful. She'd show him a cheerful face and say something polite. *Thanks, Logan. You made a crummy weekend very pleasant, and I enjoyed being with you.* She sipped her wine, ignoring the conversation that had, thank God, moved on to tomorrow's outing. After a second, she glanced at him—damn her that she couldn't keep her eyes away.

His brows had drawn together, and his eyes were focused on her face.

Chapter Eleven

"Hey, Rebecca, want to go for a walk?" Matt asked, obviously having lain in wait until after the kitchen cleanup. "I'd like to talk for a minute or two."

Rebecca glanced around the big lodge hall. Logan had disappeared, and Brandon and Paul sat by the fire, their eyes on her, looking all too interested. Darned if she wanted to stay here. "Sure." She grabbed her jacket on the way out the door.

They walked for a while in silence, and then Matt cleared his throat. "I've been thinking... Maybe I was too rough on you, about the swinging stuff and all. You... I guess I shouldn't have expected you to jump right in."

Well, this sounded more like the guy she'd moved in with, the one who was a pretty nice man. Maybe no man had manners when in hot pursuit of a woman, especially one like Ashley. Rebecca realized the sense of betrayal had faded, especially since she'd indulged in sizzling sex herself. Considering they lived together, she might do well to let him make amends. "Sorry, Matt, but I'm never going to jump in. Group sex and exchanging partners just isn't my thing. It leaves me cold."

He gave a short laugh. "And from what we all heard today, you're not exactly cold." He reached out and took her hand as they turned back toward the lodge. "I've been an idiot. You think you can forgive me?"

Since his stupid behavior let her meet Logan, she probably should thank him.

Besides, in another day, they'd drive back to San Francisco, and all this would be in the past. Logan would be in the past.

The knowledge twisted deep inside her, sending up a painful ache. But she had to face the facts. Reality was that Logan showed no interest in anything except a weekend of fun. Reality was that she lived with Matt. *Reality could really bite sometimes.*

She glanced up at the man beside her. Nice, yes, but lacking the bone-deep sense of responsibility Logan had. If she'd come here with Logan, he'd ensure her safety and comfort even if she didn't go along with his wishes. How odd. In spite of believing in equal rights and that she could fight her own battles, she still wanted to know that her guy would do anything in his power to protect her.

Matthew fell short.

As they walked around the edge of the clearing, she scuffled her feet and watched the fine dust glitter in the patchy moonlight. An owl hooted in the distance, getting no answer in return.

Loneliness crept through Rebecca. No matter what happened now, she'd move out of her apartment.

As they reached the lodge again, Matt cleared his throat. "So, are you going to forgive me?"

She realized she hadn't said a word for the entire time. Oops. "Sorry, Matt." She pulled open the door to the lodge and said, "But don't worry. I—"

Her breath burst out of her as if someone had punched her in the stomach.

Across the room, Ashley straddled Logan's knees, staring over his shoulder at Rebecca and Matt. With a smug smile, she leaned forward, pressing her breasts against Logan's face. Rebecca could only see the back of Logan's head, but she could imagine the look on his face, having the sexy Ashley offering herself.

Despite the pain in her chest, Rebecca managed to move, and she stepped back onto the porch. Matt followed, and the door closed behind him.

* * *

Had she decided to join the swingers after all? Or gone back to her boyfriend? Logan scanned the lodge room and saw Matt in a small group by the fireplace, playing some touchy-feely game. No Rebecca. Logan hadn't found her outside when he made the rounds. Or in the kitchen. Or in his bed, not that she could get there without the key code.

Anger gnawed at his guts like a hungry rodent. He didn't consider himself a particularly jealous man, but territorial? Hell yes. In the fetish clubs and here, if a BDSM group rented the cabins, he might play with a sub in public. But unlike some Doms, he didn't share. Ever.

Rebecca was welcome to change men in midstream, but she could have had the courtesy to tell him. And not worry him by disappearing.

Thor at his heels, Jake wandered in the door, shrugging out of his jacket and tossing it on the hook. "Getting cold out there. Looks like a storm's moving in."

Logan grunted and bent over to scratch Thor's sides. "You seen Rebecca?"

"Nope. Lost your woman?" Jake's sense of humor had netted him frequent black eyes as a kid.

Logan just looked at him and considered giving him another.

Grinning, Jake put his hands up and backed up a step. "Sorry, bro. I haven't seen her, but didn't you say she came with Matt?"

"That's right. But he's here in the lodge."

"The lights are on in that cabin."

"The way this group swaps beds, it could be anyone in there"—Logan scratched his jaw—"but I think I'll go check it out."

"She gonna suffer for pissing you off?"

"Fuck, yes."

* * *

Well, she liked having all her stuff around again, Rebecca decided as she took another shower, shaved her legs—although what was the point of smooth skin now?—and washed her hair with her own shampoo and conditioner.

She'd felt too awkward to move her things over to Logan's rooms, and wasn't it a good thing she hadn't?

He'd be up there now, giving Ashley a ride in front of his fireplace. Her hands fisted so tight, she could feel the fingernails cut into her skin. God, how pitiful. Rebecca pulled in a breath and felt a sob welling up from deep inside her chest.

No. No crying. No one was going to see her all red-eyed tomorrow. Not the swingers, not Logan. *Show some pride, Rebecca.*

She put on her new nightgown because she deserved something special and shoved a chair closer to the woodstove. As her hair dried, she tried to concentrate on *Little Women*, but the book couldn't compete with the ugly feelings sweeping through her. The wish to claw Ashley's face off had Rebecca digging her nails into the soft book cover. Damn Logan for falling for that nasty bitch. And why did it hurt so much that he had?

She had no claim on him, and hey, he probably took women right and left. Not a swinger, true, but a virile man with—her breath huffed out—a lot of skill and experience. And why did she have so much trouble thinking of him as just a wonderful...fuck? What a typical girlie move, imagining a relationship where there was none.

Why couldn't she be gay? Or a nun?

Somebody pounded on her cabin door. She jumped, then rolled her eyes. Two men from the club had been by already, trying to interest her in some sex. Apparently she'd have to refuse them all one by one? "Not interested," she yelled. "Go away."

A key scraped in the lock, and the handle turned. Didn't Matt ever learn? She jumped to her feet. "I told you—"

Broad shoulders filled the door, and cold blue eyes shot into hers.

"Logan?" She took a step back.

"Very good," he said in a dry voice. "You do remember me. The one you've been fucking for the past two days?" He walked toward her, as unstoppable as a semi truck, and she retreated until her back hit the wall. He put a hand flat on each side of her, trapping her. He'd never looked so angry, not even when she'd been hiking alone.

"I remember you." Then she also remembered why she'd come to the cabin. Her spine straightened. "I thought you'd be"—she spit the word at him—"*fucking* Ashley tonight."

"Ashley?" His brows drew together as if he was perplexed. "Oh, the horny blonde. I wouldn't fuck that..." Suddenly the anger disappeared from his face, and his lips curved. "You saw her jump on me and thought I'd be occupied tonight?"

Why did she have the feeling she was one step behind him? "Well, yes. If she didn't smother you with her breasts," she said drily.

"You must have been in and out within seconds, then, little one," he said softly, moving closer until she could feel the heat from his body through her thin nightgown. "Right after she shoved her tits in my face, I stood up. I'm not sure what hit harder, her ass or her pride."

Rebecca choked on a laugh and tried to contain the heady feeling sweeping through her. He'd turned Ashley down. He'd come looking for her.

"Seems like we had a bit of miscommunication here." His hand cupped her chin. "I thought you decided to go bed-hopping tonight."

"Ew." She wrinkled her nose. "Please."

His grin flashed, dark and wicked. "Then you're not all dressed up to...ah, entertain?" His gaze swept down her figure, and she became acutely aware of how very thin and provocative her nightgown appeared. Leaning a forearm against the wall over her head, he ran his other hand down her neck, across the lacy cleavage of the gown. "Very nice."

She brought her arms up and crossed them over her chest. "I put the gown on just for me." She bit her lip and added, "I felt a bit unhappy."

"Ah." The crease appeared in his cheek. "In that case, perhaps you need cheering up." He took a firm grip on her wrists and lowered her arms to her sides. "Leave them there, little sub," he cautioned.

"I'm not a—"

"Silence."

The snapped command sent heat pooling inside her as if he'd touched her.

He stroked a finger down her neck and across the top of the nightgown. She knew the sheer gold fabric wouldn't hide the tightening of her nipples. Shoot, it didn't hide anything. She'd bought it assuming she'd be somewhat toasted and with Matt, not sober and with someone who curled her toes every time she looked at him.

"Do you know how gorgeous you are?" he murmured, dipping his hand into the bodice to fondle her breast.

She stiffened. She'd thought better of him. "Don't try to snow me, Logan. I'm overweight and—"

"Becca, if you were skinny, you wouldn't have these." His hand cupped under her breast, his thumb rubbing her nipple in a way that made her legs weaken. His other hand slid down her back and curved under her bottom, pulling her against a thick erection. "I'm a big man, sugar. When I come down on a woman, I want soft, not a bundle of sticks that I might break." He leaned his weight on her. "If I want somewhere to lay my head—or the rest of me—I prefer a pillow to a rock." His hand massaged her bottom. "You, little rebel, are a pillow, and I want you just like this."

Come to think about it, Logan wouldn't bother with lies. If he didn't like something, he wouldn't be tactful about it. Conversely, if he said he liked something, she might be able to believe him. An odd feeling trickled through her as she tried to see herself through his eyes, tried to change the word *soft* from something derogatory to something of value. She was *soft* and desirable.

The door handle rattled, and a man said loudly, "Rebecca. I brought over some wine."

Logan bit her shoulder, a sharp pain that made her jump and yet wakened a throb down below. He lifted his head. "Noisy cabin you have here. You should complain to the management."

She snorted a laugh. "I'll just do that." Grasping Logan's arms, she stood on tiptoes to call over his shoulder, "Sorry, but I'm occupied."

"The management suggests a different cabin," Logan said in her ear. "One where disobedient hands can be properly restrained." He removed her hands from his arms and brought them to his mouth. As he nibbled her fingers, she couldn't help but remember how his lips had felt moving on her pussy. When he bit the soft flesh just below her thumb, a sizzle shot straight to her clit. "Let's go, sugar."

"O-okay." If she could walk that far. "Just let me change, and I'll—"

"No, I like what you're wearing." He glanced around the cabin. "Pack your suitcase."

Oh sure, like she'd parade through the lodge room in a nightgown? She'd pack, sure. And then she'd change. Tossing the suitcase on the bed, she put her things away, leaving out a pair of jeans and a shirt. Come to think of it, she couldn't walk into the lodge carrying a suitcase. She might as well wear a sign saying I'M A SLUT. She glanced at Logan. "I'm going to leave my bag here on the porch and pick it up in the morning."

His eyes crinkled, and she saw laughter lighten his blue eyes before he tossed her over his shoulder.

She struggled to find the breath he'd knocked out of her. "Hey!"

With an arm across her thighs, securing her in place, he walked out of the cabin as easily as if he had a purse over his shoulder and not a woman. He set something down, pulled the door shut, and picked it up. Her suitcase. He'd taken her suitcase, obviously intending to march into the lodge. Her suitcase and her in a sheer nightgown over his shoulder.

"Put me down. You are not going to display me like some prize you won." She squirmed on his shoulder, kicking her legs up.

His grip tightened. With a low chuckle, he said, "You know, I can carry you and your suitcase if you're quiet. If you fight, I'll need both hands, and the easiest way to keep a woman over your shoulder is with a hand on her ass, and the other hand between her legs. Your choice, pet."

Oh God, he wouldn't.

He would.

She let her body go limp.

"Wise choice." He resumed walking down the trail, swinging her suitcase at his side. "But the other way would have been more fun."

The lodge was noisy when they entered, and Rebecca kept her head down. Maybe he'd get to his door without anyone noticing.

He slammed the lodge door, and the room went silent. He strolled over to the door to upstairs.

Rebecca squeezed her eyes shut. *Macho jerk. Asshole, macho jerk.*

Boots sounded on the wooden floor. "Let me just get our door for you, bro." Jake's voice shook with laughter. The keypad beeped; the door squeaked slightly as it opened.

"Thanks." Logan turned to the swingers. He patted her butt. "Mine." His voice had a violent edge she didn't recognize, but the threatening tone came through loud and clear. "And I don't share."

Up the stairs. Into his room. By the time he tossed her onto the couch in his living room, she still hadn't found an adequate way to make him suffer before he died.

Chapter Twelve

Logan watched as his little sub struggled back to a sitting position, her green eyes all but spitting at him. "You...you Neanderthal. I don't belong to you, and you—"

Fuck, but she was adorable. Still, she was in his quarters now. He wouldn't do a submissive any favors by allowing her to get away with disrespect. Training time. "You do not have permission to speak," he growled, pleased when her tirade cut off midsentence, showing the instinctive obedience of a sub under command.

He studied her for a long minute, watching her anticipation increase as well as her worry. Her face pinkened with the beginning of arousal. Her hands rubbed her thighs, as if trying to reassure herself.

"Strip."

Her gasp was delightful. "Now, listen—"

Leaning forward, he lifted her chin so she could see his displeasure. "The only words I want from you are 'yes, Sir.' Am I clear?"

He could see her consider running, using her safe word. Then a quiver ran through her, jiggling her breasts, emphasizing the tight peaks of her nipples, and telling him her decision even before he heard her, "yes, Sir."

"Good girl." He gentled his grip, stroking her soft cheek. He kissed her, letting her feel his warmth.

The pleasure of a submissive at her master's approval glowed in her eyes when he drew back. He squeezed her shoulder, then stepped back, crossed his arms, and waited.

Biting her lip, she rose and pulled her nightgown off, laying it over the arm of the couch. Her flush increased, mostly from embarrassment.

"Take your position over there," he said, pointing to the rug by the fireplace.

She knelt as ordered. When she looked up at him through her eyelashes, he frowned until she opened her legs wider, wide enough to catch glimpses of her pussy lips within the pubic hair. Pretty, pink treats.

"Very nice, sugar. Stay there now." He pulled his toy bag out of the closet. "We're going to explore trust first. And then there are other things I want to do to you."

Her nipples tightened, and the faint glistening of her pussy showed her reaction. Since her eyes were obediently lowered, he permitted himself a grin. As he rummaged through the bag, she stayed in position. His good little sub.

The clothespin breast clamps? Not attractive enough for tonight. He moved them aside. The clover clamps? No. Too painful for her second time. Hmmm. If he used the tweezer-style, he could adjust the pinch. After a minute, he found a pair where the dangling crystals matched the green in her eyes. "Come over here."

When she stood in front of him, he smiled. "Hands behind your back again, eyes down, legs slightly apart."

He moved close enough to see the rapid beat of the pulse in her neck. "I like jewelry on my subs." Bending, he took one nipple in his mouth, sucked it to a peak, and applied a clamp, adjusting it until he saw the muscles around her eyes tighten with pain. Appreciation swept through him; she wasn't a whiner, was she? He pulled the ring down to loosen the clamp slightly. Her teeth nibbled her lips again, so he kissed her and checked her pussy. Very wet. The other clamp went on, accompanied by a hiss of breath. He slid his fingers back into her pussy again, tracing her folds, increasing her arousal.

Her body quivered uncontrollably as Logan fondled her, sliding his fingers over her clit until it throbbed. When he pushed a finger inside her, she had to clench her hands to stay still. With her eyes lowered, she could only see his long legs and his muscular forearm, the sleeves of his rolled-up shirt, his corded wrist, and the hand touching her so intimately.

Touching her as if she had no right to deny him.

Her nipples burned from the clamps. An intense sensation, never lessening, it seemed to make everything on her body more sensitive.

"Bend over and spread your cheeks."

Her head came up, and she stared at him. "What?"

His eyebrows drew together, his eyes turning cold. "Try again, sub."

No no no. Whatever he wanted to do, this couldn't be good. "No. I won't. I don't want whatever you're going to do."

"Do you know what I'm going to do, Becca?"

She shook her head. "But—"

"Do you think it will hurt you unbearably?"

"No, but—"

"Have you ever been raped or assaulted?"

"No, but—"

"Then you're saying you don't trust me to do what I think is right for you. Is that it?"

"Dammit, Logan, you can't just do stuff to me without asking me!" She stomped, but her bare foot didn't make a sound.

"Yes. I can." His jaw tightened, and a quaking started inside her. "That's what domination is all about. And it's something you want, but you're too afraid to relinquish control. That control is what I'm taking away from you, one step at a time."

She couldn't look away from the intense blue of his eyes, and despite the chill in the air, she could feel a sweat break out over her body.

"Now, either use your safe word and we will stop, or say, 'Yes, Sir,' and do as I ordered. And take the punishment that comes with your defiance."

She didn't want to stop. No. She wanted him to hold her and say he would do what she wanted. She wanted his hands on her, not something in her butt.

No expression on his face, he waited, looking down at her, making her feel small. Naked.

Just standing next to him made tremors run through her until the jewelry on her breasts jingled softly. She thought of his strong fingers attaching the clamps...his touch. Even as her mind screamed no, she sighed. "Yes, Sir." She turned and bent slightly.

A growl of exasperation, then his powerful hand grasped the nape of her neck, pressing inexorably down until she could almost touch the floor. "Spread your cheeks. Now."

Her breath came in small pants of humiliation as she moved her hands to her bottom.

He squirted a cold liquid between her cheeks. Then something pressed against her rectum, trying to slide inside, and she whined, "Noooo."

One of his hands pressed against her mound, the other inserted the...the thing. It slid in, stretching her rectum, and seemed to plop in. She could feel it inside her. Foreign and hard.

"This is called an anal plug, sugar," he murmured. "It opens a whole new set of nerves and also stretches you a tad. I'm not going to take you there, not this weekend. You're too tight, and I'm too big. But this gives you an idea of what it would feel like." He pulled her hands down, and she realized her fingernails had been digging in her buttocks. "Stand up now."

Her cheeks closed over the plug, and it felt as if she had a rock between her buttocks. She shifted uncomfortably.

He moved to her front and wrapped a belt around her waist, yanking it snug. A piece of leather dangled from it. She looked at him questioningly.

He chuckled. "You'll see." His voice softened, and he caressed her cheek. "I'm glad you're still here, Becca. I know this is scary, especially for you. You're a woman who likes everything under her control."

Warmth filled her. He knew she was scared. He understood that and understood her.

And then he took a dildo out of his bag, and she backed away so quickly that she tripped.

He grabbed her by the wrist. "Nope, you're not moving. This is what you earned with your defiance." It looked horrible. Shaped like a Y, one arm was the traditional phallic shape, and the other was shorter with a pointy end. "You ever used a rabbit?"

She shook her head. She had an old vibrator she'd picked up in college from a porn store. Ancient. And it lived somewhere in the bathroom.

"Spread your legs, sugar."

He'd stuck something up her butt, and now he wanted to stuff something else into her? And why did his patient waiting drive her into doing what he wanted? She spread her legs, closing her eyes in humiliation.

The damn thing slid in easily. She was horribly wet, and he had to have noticed. As he adjusted it, she realized the short leg of the Y would be positioned right over her clit. Smiling slightly, he brought the leather between her legs and fit the end of the vibrator into a small hole. He tightened the leather, pushing everything up inside her even more, and secured it to the belt. "Good enough." He smiled into her eyes, then arched a brow. "A mite upset, sweetie?"

She glared at him. "May I talk now?"

He studied her for a minute. "Nope. You'll say something I can't overlook, and you've already got one punishment coming. Go in the kitchen and get us both some water. Use the red glasses."

How could she walk with this stuff in her?

He raised an eyebrow.

Damn, damn, damn. She knew she was walking bowlegged. With every movement, the rabbit thing rubbed against her clit and the anal thing moved inside her. And somehow it all started to turn her on.

She found red glasses—plastic ones—and got the water. On the way back to the living room, suddenly the rabbit came alive. The thing pulsed and rippled in her vagina. Over her clit, it vibrated. It seemed to bump against the anal plug, and she felt everything inside her coiling tighter and tighter, so fast and fierce, she barely had time for a breath before she came in a mind-blowing orgasm.

When her vision cleared, she realized the vibrations had stopped. And somehow she'd managed to hold on to the glasses. She wobbled back into the living room.

Logan sat on the couch, arm over the back, watching her. "Iron control. Very impressive, sugar."

Scowling, she handed him a glass, trembling so violently, the water splashed over the rim. "You did that on purpose."

His jaw tightened slightly at her nasty tone. He pointed to the rug beside the fireplace. "Over there. Slave position."

She started to ask him to remove the things now he'd made his point. His stern expression warned her against it. In front of the fireplace, she eased to the floor. The kneeling position pushed everything up higher inside her and rubbed the front arm of the rabbit against her swollen clit.

She stared at the rug, her body so sensitive, her skin seemed able to feel him approach. His feet appeared in the small circle of rug where her eyes had focused.

He walked behind her and buckled wrist cuffs on her. The inside of the snugly fitting cuffs were soft with fur. He clipped the cuffs together. "Sugar, I don't want you to move, to speak, or to look up. Any infraction will result in you spending more time here. The cuffs are to help."

Help? He didn't think she could sit still and keep her hands behind her back? She huffed a breath and gave a mental shrug. As punishments went, this wasn't so bad. She didn't mind kneeling.

She heard the couch creak, then the sound of pages of a book being turned...and a hum as the vibrator inside her turned on. She managed to keep from gasping. In this position, she could feel every vibration course through her. The part of the rabbit just inside her labia rippled, and the front arm made a tapping sensation right over her clit. Arousal shot through her, and her insides coiled as she approached an orgasm. Oh God, oh God. But she could handle it and not move. She kept her eyes down, her back stiffening as—

Everything stopped. Surprise rolled through her, followed by frustration. Her body hovered right on the edge. Held by the cuffs, her hands fisted. Then relaxed as the pressure of the stalled climax receded.

Heavy footsteps thudded outside Logan's quarters, coming up the stairs. A knock. The door opened, and Rebecca closed her eyes. She waited for Logan to shove the person back out the door. To say something. Or cover her.

He did nothing.

Horrified, she looked up to see Logan's brother just inside the door. She stared at him in disbelief. She was naked, damn it! Naked with breast clamps and objects inserted into her. Embarrassment paralyzed her legs, or she'd have fled.

As she gaped at Jake, his face turned dark with disapproval. "Eyes down, sub," he snapped with the same authority as Logan...or a Dom.

She averted her gaze from him, looking at Logan instead.

He was watching her, and his eyes were gray. Cold. He tapped his watch. "Another ten minutes added on."

Oh God. Oh God. Oh God. She dropped her gaze, the heat of humiliation making her feel as if she sat in a sauna. How could Logan do this to her?

"Very pretty pet you got there, bro," Jake said. "Not trained very well, though. You got a minute, or is this a bad time?"

"I'm not busy for a while. Sit."

Sit? He invited his brother to sit? Now fury alternated with the embarrassment. She clenched her jaw against the need to scream at Logan. And his brother.

And then the vibrator turned back on. She squeezed her eyes shut, trying not to react, not to show anything for the bastards, damn them. Her body heated, jumping straight to the precipice despite Jake's presence. Her hands tightened into fists as her focus narrowed to the thing over her clit, to the coursing, pulsing, almost there...

Everything stopped.

The tiny moan escaped her. She stayed frozen. She couldn't believe he'd done it to her again. And he didn't even seem to be paying attention to her. She could hear the men's low conversation now that her ears had stopped ringing.

"Gonna collar her, bro?"

Logan snorted as if Jake had said something funny. "I'm no full-time master."

"It can just mean commitment. You know, going steady."

What the heck was a collar? she wondered. Like a dog? Who was Jake talking about?

"Enough, asshole," Logan growled. "Not going to happen."

"Your loss." And Jake started talking about a series of storms due tomorrow and plans for the club members.

As their discussion continued, Rebecca slowly brought her breathing back under control although her entire pussy burned.

A few minutes later, the vibrator turned back on.

And just before she came, it clicked off. Again. And on. And off.

At some point, she realized Jake had left. *On. Off.* Her body trembled continuously. If her hands had been free, she would have attacked Logan. Everything throbbed painfully. Past painfully. If she could only come... She shifted, trying to rub the vibrator more against her clit, just a—

"If you move, I add more time." His voice deep, even. No emotion.

What kind of emotion would he have when she killed him dead? When she strung his guts from the trees and—

On.

When the vibrator stopped, she couldn't keep the moan back, let alone the tears that spilled from her closed eyes. She shook so hard, she wasn't sure she'd ever stop.

Callused hands closed on each side of her face, the warmth startling. "Eyes on me, Becca."

She looked up, her vision blurry from tears. His face was still cold, mean. She didn't like him this way.

"When under command, who do you obey, Becca?" His words seemed to cut through her.

"You," she whispered, adding a hasty "Sir" when his jaw tightened.

"Do you need to worry or think about anything when I'm in control?"

"No, Sir."

"What is left for that head of yours to do, then, sugar?"

Her mind blanked. If he had all the control, and she didn't think, what was left?

"Just feel, Becca. That's all that's left."

The shock rolling through her was as overwhelming as the whole evening had been. No power, no control, no need to worry or think. All she had left was what she'd just experienced. Sensation. The trembling increased inside her, and she closed her eyes.

He walked behind her and unsnapped her cuffs. After bringing her arms forward, he leaned her back against his legs, and his strong hands massaged the ache out of her shoulders. Her hands in her lap shook almost as violently as her emotions. From feeling so vulnerable to being cared for; she couldn't keep up. She didn't want to keep up.

Her eyes opened when he lifted her into his arms. She looked at him, his jaw a rigid line, his neck all corded muscle, and she felt fragile, and even more, safe in his embrace.

He carried her to his bed and laid her on her stomach. She turned her head to watch him.

Standing close, he stroked her hair. "Punishment's over. You did well, Becca. I'm pleased with you." His smile of approval warmed the coldness inside her.

Gripping her hips, he tilted her onto her knees, head on the mattress, and buckled on ankle cuffs. Pulling her arms around, he clipped each wrist cuff to an ankle cuff, restraining her in that position. A shudder went through her as she realized he wasn't through with her.

When he removed the vibrator, she almost screamed as just the movement inside shot her straight back into arousal. His fingers circled her clit, sliding in the wetness. She whimpered as the nub tightened unbearably. "All red and swollen," he murmured. "Just right."

She shook her head, tears blurring her eyes again.

Cupping her cheek, he kissed her gently. "What, Becca? What's wrong?"

"I can't do it again. Please don't...not again."

A crease appeared in his cheek even as heat grew in his eyes. "We won't stop this time, and you're going to come so hard that the swingers will hear you in their cabins."

He stripped completely, and her eyes widened as his cock sprang out, long and thick. He wrapped his hand around it at the base. "You weren't the only one suffering, sweetie."

After sheathing himself in a condom, he knelt behind her and pressed his chest against her back. His body felt heavy and warm. The gentle bobbing of his cock against her folds made her jump.

His hand slid down her stomach, over her mound, and then his fingers slid in circles around her core. She moaned as the excruciating tightness increased. His cock pressed against her opening, up and down, slickening with her wetness, teasing her opening.

Then he ruthlessly pinched her sensitive clit even as he thrust his thick cock up into her.

She screamed as every stymied climax tore through her at once. Her eyes blinded, she arched. Explosion after explosion ripped her body into pieces with exquisite, terrifying pleasure.

His fingers released her as he slid his cock in and out. She spasmed around the hard length, and another wave of pleasure rippled through her. Her heart hammered inside her chest so brutally, it felt close to bursting. Somehow the air in the room had disappeared. She gasped for air.

Wrapping an arm around her stomach, he started into the merciless, driving rhythm she was becoming used to.

Only somehow it seemed more intense. As his pelvis pressed against her bottom, she realized why. He'd left that plug in her. Every thrust inside her moved it slightly, filled her fuller, and sent odd feelings thrumming through her. Sensations she didn't know. Ones she didn't want to like...but she did. Oh God, she did.

She was so hot and wet, he wanted to just bury himself deep and let himself come. But he had one more thing to accomplish. So he throttled himself down, moving his cock in and out very, very slowly, giving her a chance to recover. But damn, she'd better recover fast. This position was hell on a man's control.

Trying to divert himself, he slid his hand beneath her breasts. God, they were gorgeous, so full they spilled over his hand, and her nipples so sensitive that any tug on the clamps made her pussy clench around him.

Gradually he angled himself so his cock would hit harder over her G-spot. He grinned when she stiffened. Apparently he'd hit the right spot, one as sensitive as her breasts.

Obviously forgetting her restraints, she moaned and tried to move, halted by the cuffs. Her vagina clenched around him as she realized her vulnerability. Her iron control was in tatters, her will given over to him, even as her body was his.

He pushed her legs farther apart to emphasize her helplessness and saw her hands close into fists. *Fists.* He hadn't reached the naked core of her submission yet. Gripping the chains of the breast clamps, he tugged gently with each thrust. Reading her and responding accordingly, pushing her toward pure sensation and submission even as he drove her body to climax, reminded him of how Beethoven's symphonies ended when all the parts came together in the finale.

She slowly tightened around him. Her thighs, widely apart, trembled like aspen leaves in a winter wind, but the restraints kept her legs from giving out. She was close.

Pushing back to a kneeling position, he slid his hand down her stomach to her pussy, anchoring her in place and putting pressure on her distended clit at the same time. With the other hand, he grasped the slender butt plug in her vulnerable little ass. He wiggled it, increasing the sensation, increasing her submission.

Her whole body quivered in shock, and she made an indescribable noise. Her hips jerked, inadvertently rubbing her swollen nub against his restraining hand. She whimpered, yielding to the pleasure. *To him.* Only a Dom could know and appreciate this rushing sense of power.

He thrust with his cock and slid the soft plug out; he pulled his cock out and pushed the plug in. Her legs turned rigid, her back arching, thrusting her bottom up higher. As he continued, her silky pussy clamped down on him, tighter and tighter, and seconds later she convulsed, wailing her climax in short cries that corresponded with each rippling spasm of her vagina. Fuck, he loved her unrestrained response, and even more, that she needed restraints to get there.

The tight milking sensation around his cock grew until he couldn't stand it anymore. He seated the butt plug firmly inside her, grasped her hips with both hands, and pounded into her. His own climax boiled up and out of him like a volcano, the fire coming from deep within and shooting through him.

When he could breathe again, he released the clips holding her wrists to her ankles and toppled them both over, pulling her up against him so her back rested against his chest. He was still embedded deep inside her. Would that he could stay there forever. Wrapping his arms around her, he buried his face in her silky hair. God, he enjoyed having a soft, shuddering sub in his arms.

And this soft little sub had just gifted him with a depth of response that awed him. Such a change from her assertiveness during the day. Damn, he liked that. Liked her cheerful personality—even at breakfast, for which she should be shot. And the way she petted Thor, even when he scared her. The way she smiled when she saw a doe and fawn. The way her big green eyes had looked at him when she gave him her wrists.

He wanted *this* soft little sub, and he wanted his collar around her neck. God help him.

* * *

Short crackling bursts of fire from M-16s like firecrackers on steroids. The earth-jarring blast of an IED. The truck humps into the air, spilling him and the others like marbles across the concrete. Screaming...so much screaming. Sweat pours down his face, or maybe the hot liquid is blood. Heart hammering, he dodges across the alley, dives into a building. His helmet has disappeared somewhere. The even, thudding noise of a fifty cal opens up, then the roar of a MedEvac helicopter. He turns to look, knowing what he'll see. Too late for rescue. His team, oh God, his team. Red streaks the sand like a blood-filled kaleidoscope. Shrieks of agony. Men pour across the alley, coming for him. His hands tighten on the—

"Logan!"

Hands shook him, tiny hands. He grabbed the soldier's arms. Soft, round. The voice wasn't right, high, using his name. He blinked and saw big green eyes, pale skin with freckles, pink, pink lips. He forced his hands to loosen. "Becca." His voice sounded like he'd scraped it raw.

"Are you awake now?" She smoothed his hair back from his sweaty face. "That sounded like one nasty nightmare."

His breath huffed out. "Yeah." His hands tightened on her shoulders, red still staining the edges of his vision. What had he done? Had he hit her? "Are you all right?"

"Well, sure. I wasn't the one having a nightmare." She pushed out of his arms and trotted into the bathroom; the last two burning candles glinted off her pale skin.

He sighed, his insides churning worse now that present-day horror had been added. God, how could he have fallen asleep? He could have—

"Here." An arm under his shoulders urged him up. He took the glass she gave him and stared at it.

"Logan, drink it."

Cold water cleared the dryness from his throat. After setting the glass on the bedside stand, she washed the sweat from his face and chest with a washcloth. "There."

Before he found the words to tell her he needed to leave, she pushed him back down and curled up next to him, laying her head on his shoulder. One rounded arm curved over his chest, holding him gently. "I hate nightmares," she murmured and fell asleep within two breaths.

Logan stared up at the ceiling, too aware of the woman snuggled up to him like a trusting puppy. Already sound asleep. After a minute, he put a hand under his head and wrapped the other around her shoulders. Stronger than she looked, wasn't she? Considering her description of the dog attack, she probably knew all about nightmares.

She sure dealt with them a hell of a lot better than he did. He'd never done anything afterward except sit on the edge of the bed and shake. The water she'd given him had washed away more than the dryness, the washcloth more than sweat, somehow grounding him in reality and banishing the usual lingering remnants.

Her breath created a tiny warm patch on his shoulder as her chest rose and fell in the peaceful rhythm of sleep.

He took a long, careful breath. He'd been lucky and hadn't hurt her. There would be no sleep for him tonight, but contentment could be found in the here and now.

Chapter Thirteen

Rebecca checked the sausage and the egg dishes in the oven. Almost time for the biscuits to go in.

"How can you do this alone when everyone else needs help?" Logan asked, tucking an arm around her waist and pulling her back against his chest.

His deep voice and firm touch made a shiver run down her spine right to her toes. "Lots of practice feeding starving frat boys."

He kissed the juncture of her shoulder, his day-old whiskers scratchy and his lips warm. "Barefoot and in the kitchen. A man's favorite dream except there's too many people around to toss you on the table, put your legs over my shoulders, and take you before breakfast."

She quivered inside and outside, turning her head to glance at the big kitchen island table. "Ah, right. Way too many people." Her voice came out husky.

Pushing aside the top of her flannel shirt, he bit her shoulder, then squeezed her bottom, reminding her of what had been inside her last night. How it had made her feel. She almost moaned.

Logan chuckled. "I'll get out of your way, unless there's something you'd like me to do."

"No. I have it handled." She finished frying the sausage for the gravy, enjoying the sizzling sound, before turning around. He'd taken a stool by the island, all big male in a dark blue T-shirt. When he moved, his biceps stretched the sleeves in a way that made her mouth dry. So darned gorgeous, but... She frowned. The lines around his eyes seemed deeper, darker. "You look tired. Did you have trouble sleeping after your nightmare?"

He winced and then gave her a faint smile. "With you in my bed, I sleep far too easily."

Was that an answer or not? Didn't like talking about his nightmares, maybe? She sure could understand that.

The smell of the sausage forced her attention to cooking. By the time she'd started the gravy and popped biscuits into the oven, chatter and laughter drifted in from the dining room. Jenna and Brandy came in for dishes to set the tables, chattering about their night, giving Rebecca and Logan sidelong looks as if they wanted to ask about their night also.

Like Rebecca would talk about the stuff she'd done, let alone what *he'd* done to her.

Even before Logan had showed up, her abused nipples and clit had tingled and ached with each brush of her clothing. And having Logan in the same room somehow made every inch of her skin more sensitive.

Trying to ignore her body, she pulled the egg casseroles out of the oven and put the bacon onto a platter. The biscuits went into a covered basket.

With a low hum of pleasure, Logan nudged her to one side so he could snag himself a couple of biscuits. After kissing her cheek—and nipping her earlobe—he retreated back to the table. She grinned and shook her head. The jerk. Now her body was really awake. If the man didn't leave her alone, she'd start wailing and rubbing on everything like a cat in heat.

Concentrate, girl. Eyes on the food, she poured gravy into another bowl just as people streamed into the kitchen. She pointed out the bowls and platters and stood aside as they carried the food away. When Mel peeked in the door, Rebecca lifted her hands. "That's it. Go eat."

"Great," Mel said, patting his ample belly. "It looks fantastic, Rebecca. You're a hell of a cook."

"Thanks." She grabbed the bacon she'd saved and treated Thor, who waited patiently at his spot inside the door. A hug and lick later, she joined Logan at the island. "Aren't you going to eat?"

"In a minute," Logan said, not looking up. Her eyes widened when she saw what occupied his attention. She'd left her sketchbook on the table. Damn.

When her hand snaked out to pull it back, his fingers closed on her wrist, holding her in place with an ease that made her panties wet. Darn it, he shouldn't be able to affect her like this, especially with some macho, strong-man tactic.

His steel blue gaze met hers, and her stomach took a ride down an elevator without a bottom floor. Never mind the strength...his effect on her was born from his sheer competence, the authority in his gaze, and his easy assumption that she'd obey.

His lips curved. "Are you one of those creative types that doesn't share her work until it's finished?"

She wet her lips. She tried to tug her arm and got nowhere except to increase the heat sizzling through her veins. "Ah, right. I don't share."

His eyes narrowed. "You've never lied to me before, sugar. Don't start now." He rose and towered over her, taking her chin and forcing her to meet his gaze. "Truth, please."

"Damn you." And damn her telltale coloring, which had undoubtedly turned red. "I drew stuff that...that's embarrassing, okay?"

"Ah." The devil probably had a grin just like that. "Now I definitely have to look." He curved an arm around her waist and pulled her up against him as he sat back down on the stool, flipping the pages.

Landscapes at first, Paul and Amy sunning on the rocks at the lake, scenes from Yosemite, the waterfalls. One of Jake squatting at the edge of a creek, lecturing about fish. Logan behind his desk, cold and implacable, just like the first time she'd seen him. He grinned at that, flipped the page, and let out a shout of laughter.

Ashley with tits so big she had to hold them up and a bladelike nose over collagen-gone-wild lips. "Remind me to never piss you off, sweetheart."

Another of Logan in his Dom mode, power almost shimmering off the page. A deer with a fawn peeking from behind its legs.

Logan sighed and took her hand. "You can draw like this, and you do advertising instead?"

His question increased her resolve to think about her life, but he didn't harass her or try to talk her into something, just raised the question and let it drop.

Two pictures of Thor—one drawn how she'd originally seen him as a growling, terrifying monster, and one she'd done yesterday with his happy grin, tongue lolling half out. Logan tapped that one. "Sell me this."

Finally something she could give him back. Reaching across him, she tore it out of the pad. "It's yours."

His eyebrows rose.

"Consider it payment for the...lessons." Okay, she'd started blushing again.

He pulled her between his legs, trapping her between unyielding thighs. His hands tightened around her waist, sending a tremor through her. "You think I need payment for what happened between us?" Brows together, eyes narrowed, obviously displeased.

"Uh. Nope, guess not." Her legs wobbled when his hands slid up to graze her breasts. "How about it's a present because I..." *Enjoyed the sex?* She slammed her mouth shut and tried again. "Because we're friends?" But more than friends. Really. Weren't they?

"That will work, little rebel," he murmured. His lips curved up. "If you don't want to try out the table, right here and now, I suggest you go eat your breakfast." His jeans bulged with a thick erection.

It took a major effort to pull back, and another one to make her shaky legs go in a straight direction.

* * *

Logan had disappeared into his rooms for part of the morning, then reappeared and talked Rebecca into helping with trail repairs. But they'd had to stop when a storm hit, whipping the trees and whistling around the lodge. Rain poured down in what the frat mother from Texas would have called a gully-washer.

Logan asked if she wanted to drive into town with him, but she'd been too enchanted by the storm, so she and Thor had huddled together on the lodge porch while the tempest raged. After the rain stopped and Thor had trotted away, undoubtedly to investigate some doggy thing, she'd spent a lovely few hours painting, trying to capture the eerie sunlight sliding through the dark clouds overhead.

The quiet time gave her a chance to think over what had happened yesterday…and last night. Logan had tied her up. And she liked it. He'd punished her, and she didn't like it, but even that had aroused her. Logan had let Jake see her naked, and okay, that still bothered her. But not enough for her not to have come, obviously, since she had. She'd think she'd gone insane, except Logan said an amazingly high number of people got off on dominance and submission. And bondage. The whole BDSM route.

She scowled. Logan, the man, made her hot. Logan, the Dom, turned the heat to incandescent. Just the thought of how he restrained her and took her, not giving her any choice in…in anything, made her wet. Really wet.

Okay, Rebecca. Paint. Don't think. Just paint.

When she finally put her art supplies away, she realized she was smiling. All the nerves from her job—and from the swingers—had been silenced, and she simply felt *content*.

But she needed to start supper. Tonight she'd planned a simple Italian menu: spaghetti, salad, and garlic bread. She pulled the sausage out of the refrigerator and started it to brown, then opened the back door for Thor.

No Thor.

She stepped outside and inhaled the fresh air, looking around for the dog. How odd. He always waited at the back door, well before every meal. Logan hadn't taken the dog, and Jake had led some club members up an easterly trail to snap pictures of rainbows. When Thor left after the rain, the dog had gone up the trail to the west.

Where could he be?

After turning the sausage, she checked the door again. And again. And again. By the time the spaghetti simmered in a giant pot, she couldn't stand waiting anymore. Jake said Thor never missed a meal…ever. Something must be wrong.

She went into the main room. Almost empty except for three men playing cards.

"I call," Mel growled.

Paul scowled at him and then glanced up at Rebecca. "Something wrong?"

"Maybe. Thor hasn't come back, and he's always here for meals."

"Thor?" Christopher's brows drew together. "We don't have anyone named Thor."

"It's the dog, idiot." Mel patted Rebecca's arm. "He's probably out chasing a deer or something. I wouldn't worry."

"But Jake says he always—"

"Let's see what you've got, you bastard." Mel tapped the table, and the men's attention turned to the cards. She'd obviously been dismissed.

Kicking over the table won't help. Might be satisfying but won't help. She walked to the front door and onto the porch, scowling at the surrounding mountains. Miles and miles of forest. Sunset arrived in about two hours. That didn't leave her much time, but she could at least walk up the trail a ways.

Okay, then. She crossed the clearing and the rutted dirt road, her sneakers squishing noisily in the mud. When she moved into the forest, the temperature dropped at least ten degrees, and the moist pine needles added a sharp scent to the clean tang of the air. Stopping only to call Thor's name, she followed the trail as it switched back and forth, climbing steadily upward. Stillness surrounded her, with only an occasional creak of overhead branches accompanied by a spatter of rainwater, the cry of a distant hawk, and the rushing sound of a nearby stream. Was this what peace sounded like?

Her heart and lungs had adapted to the higher altitude over the past few days, so her body felt good, like a well-functioning machine. And the machine had lost the feeling of coiled tension. As she thought of returning to work on Thursday, to meetings and pressure, to power plays and pissing contests, her stomach twisted.

She reached a small rocky outlook and stopped to enjoy the warmth of the sun and catch her breath. Over the higher mountains in the east, dark clouds lingered, the sheeting rain a glorious golden from the setting sun. A tiny question poked up inside her, a tendril of a thought. If she didn't like the thought of returning to work, was that an indication of vacationitis or something deeper?

She turned and glanced at the sun. No time to stop and think. "Thor!" she yelled, then listened. *Nothing.* She repeated it twice and then started back on the trail, still heading up.

Okay, she didn't particularly like the people aspect of her job. No, actually, she hated the people aspect. With that thought came another. Why the heck did she want to be a senior art director and be stuck with managing people? That made no sense at all. *Duh, Rebecca.* The American dream— advance or die, make more money or you're a loser—had sucked her right into its maw.

She had been more satisfied cooking meals here than almost anything she had done at her high-paid job. But she loved painting. Drawing. Sketching. The sheer creative moments. Taking a concept and making it flow. If only she didn't have to deal with inane subject matter and clients and... Face it, given a choice, she'd far rather draw for herself than for an advertising team.

She stopped dead and scowled at the winding path. What was this, *Revelation Trail?* She needed to get the heck off it before her entire career got flushed down the drain.

Too late. She pushed a branch up and ducked under it, receiving a shower of raindrops. *Interim plan.* Return to work with open eyes and see if she still felt the same way. Maybe this was just some weird mountain effect.

But if she still felt the same way. Well. She'd start looking for something closer to what she liked. The relief and anticipation that washed through her with that decision surprised her. Had she been ignoring her feelings all these years?

She startled a deer—mutual startlement really, considering she'd almost jumped out of her sneakers—and stopped at a viewpoint that made her fingers itch for her paints. Then she noticed the slant of the sun's rays. She frowned. How long had she been hiking? She needed to be able to get back by dark. "Thor," she yelled. "Thor!"

Was that a whine? She tilted her head and listened, hearing winds rustling the branches high overhead, a stream rushing somewhere below, and a whimper. God, it was him. "Where are you, guy?"

The whine came from downhill. She left the trail, heading toward a greener area, which indicated a streambed. Pushing through damp vegetation, she reached the water and stopped. "Thor. Say something."

A whine came from the other side. She spotted a hint of brown fur in a bunch of logs and branches. Oh great. Just how could she get over there? That damn water moved faster than miniature rapids. She scowled, checking up and down the stream. Did they forget to put in bridges? After a minute, she saw how the boulders poking out of the rushing water might form a traversable path...if she hopped from stone to stone.

She marked the pattern in her head and then started across. Slipped and recovered. Darn it, she was *so* not an athlete. Another rock, this one slimy with moss and spray. Another. Finally only a long leap to the bank remained. Piece of cake.

She jumped and exhilaration soared through her as she came down clear of the water, but then her foot landed on a piece of wood and skidded. Her ankle twisted, and she fell hard onto her hip and shoulder.

Dammit. Once she recovered the breath knocked out of her, she pushed herself to a sitting position. "Well, how graceful."

But she'd made it over. *Yay, team.* As she stood, her weight came down on her left foot, and pain seared through her ankle like someone had attacked her with a carving knife. Without knowing how, she ended back on her butt. "Well, dammit again." Pulling her knee up, she fingered her ankle and hissed. Swelling already. Pain throbbed through it in a heavy beat. Just a twist, surely. She'd be able to walk on it. A chill ran through her as she checked the sun. Not quite down to the treetops, but it sure seemed to have sped up its descent. *Damn, damn, damn.*

Her ankle twisted the minute she put weight on it, and red and black danced in front of her eyes like a checkerboard of pain. This was so not good. The dog's whine recalled her to her mission. "Okay, baby, I'm coming." She'd try to help him, even if she had to crawl.

Crawling sucked.

"Sheesh, Thor, couldn't have found an easier place to get trapped?" she asked as she got closer. Caught in a tangle of debris, he'd obviously fallen through the mass of downed branches. She edged onto the pile and reached down to him.

He covered her hand with dog kisses before she got him to settle down. She surveyed the situation. If she pulled away that branch and that one... She broke branches and yanked away others, giving him room to move.

He didn't.

Why? She shoved her good foot under a log and, headfirst, edged farther down into the prison of branches. A sharp, broken-off stub was jammed into Thor's paw, pinning it. Major owie. Rebecca reached down and broke off more branches until she reached the one stabbing into his paw. No way to move it without hurting him. Her muscles tight, she whispered, "Don't bite me, okay?" She yanked the branch away from his paw.

When he yipped, she cringed, yanking her hand away.

Thor didn't even snarl. Tail wagging, he clambered out of the debris pile, doing much better on three legs than she did on one.

She crawled back off, groaning each time her swollen ankle bumped a branch. A little ways from the streambed, she sat down next to a tree and leaned against the trunk. "Let's see that paw, guy."

Thor trotted over and actually held his paw up for her. A thin trickle of blood oozed from the jagged gash. *Great.* "I cannot believe I'm going to do first aid on a dog," she said to him. "You won't hurt me. Right?" She pulled off her shirt, then took off the chemise underneath. Nice and stretchy. She wrapped it around his paw, whimpering with him, and tied it in place with the shoulder straps. "There. All better," she said and received a wet lick over her cheek.

Ugh. Next job, teach him how to give verbal thank-yous.

He sat next to her, lifting his front leg with a whine.

"Yeah, me too." She ran her fingers through his soft, thick fur. "We're quite the pair. How are we ever going to get back?" She eyed the stream. Without two good legs, she couldn't jump, and even if she tried to wade, with water so fierce, she wouldn't be able to keep her feet. She sure couldn't crawl across. *Damn, damn, damn.*

Thor dropped down beside her and laid his head in her lap. His sigh joined hers.

"We are so screwed."

* * *

Logan carried an armload of groceries into the kitchen and looked around. Paul and Mel were putting dishes into the dishwasher while Christopher scrubbed pots in the sink.

Something smelled good, and he'd missed it. Damn. "Spaghetti?"

"Yes," Mel said. "It would have been really good except Rebecca bailed out, and Ashley cooked the noodles into mush."

"What do you mean, *Rebecca bailed?*"

Behind Logan, the kitchen door opened, and Jake walked in with the last sack of groceries. "I saw you were back. Is this it?"

"Yeah, thanks." Logan started unpacking the goods and putting things away. "Have you seen Rebecca?"

Jake's hand stalled over a loaf of bread. "I thought she went into town with you."

A chill slid up Logan's spine. "No, she wanted to paint." He turned to Mel. "You said she bailed. Where to?"

"Ah." Mel exchanged glances with the other two men. "She was worried about the dog, but I told her it probably took off after a deer. I—"

"I don't remember seeing her after that. 'Bout an hour ago?" Paul said, frowning at Christopher. "We didn't think too much about her not being here, since she isn't hanging with the group."

Logan rubbed his jaw and glanced at Jake. "If she was worried about Thor, she'd go after him."

Jake nodded. "That's how I read it."

Logan glanced at the swingers. "You people stay here at the lodge. I don't need anyone else lost." He didn't wait for an answer, just headed into the main room, stopping long enough to grab a heavy-duty flashlight and his backpack from the hook on the wall. Jake followed right behind him.

Outside, Logan checked at the sun, his gut tightening with fear. "Got less than an hour."

Jake grunted an answer, then walked over to the west edge of the clearing to check for tracks. Logan did the same on the east side. At the road, he found tiny tracks with shallow indentations. Sneakers on little feet. "Over here." He followed the shoe marks first, then the muddy streaks leading to the east trail.

"Nice that we've got a place to start," Jake said, following Logan into the forest. "God help us if we didn't have that."

Logan didn't bother to answer but broke into a jog. *Little rebel, what the fuck were you thinking?* But he knew. She'd thought only of the dog, not her own safety.

Dammit, she wasn't stupid. Not in the least. She'd have seen the sun setting and would have turned back. If she could. As he ran, his eyes skimmed over the forest, checking for signs of her passage. And he couldn't help but see all the ways she could be hurt. Or killed.

Chapter Fourteen

When Thor's ears perked forward, Rebecca sat up. "What?" She tilted her head and then could hear it too: a shrill sound from higher up. Another. Someone was blowing a whistle.

Oh God. Thank you, God. A sob wrenched out of her as tears overflowed her eyes. Now with hopes of rescue, she could admit how terrified she'd been.

She rubbed the wetness off her cheeks. *No wussy behavior.* It was probably Logan. After taking a slow breath, she firmed up her voice. "Here!" she yelled. "We're here."

She could see someone up high, about where she'd left the trail. A second later, Logan came down the incline in a graceful slide, Jake shortly after. They followed the path she'd broken through the streamside brush.

They stalked up to the stream, two powerful men, like two more animals that belonged here in the forest. Logan stopped at the edge of the stream for only a second before crossing on the same stones she'd used, so fast and coordinated she wanted to hit him. Jake moved just as fast.

Shoulder to shoulder, they scowled down at her.

"I hurt my ankle," she said meekly, wanting only to fling herself into Logan's arms. "And Thor hurt his foot. He got trapped in there." She pointed at the pile of river wrack.

Logan didn't speak as he knelt beside her. His eyes were cold, the muscles of his jaw rigid, and she realized he was furious. Boiling-over and ready-to-yell furious. He stared at her and then inhaled, and his anger disappeared. How did he do that? Have so much control over his emotions?

"Come here," he said softly and pulled her into his arms. Oh God. His scent surrounded her, and his arms wrapped her in security. She laid her cheek against his muscular chest and tried really, really hard not to cry. She didn't succeed very well.

"Shhh," he whispered, stroking her hair. "You're safe, sweetheart." A growl entered his voice. "For now."

After a minute, she got herself under control and reluctantly pushed back. No time to be a baby.

Logan wiped a tear off her cheek with his thumb, his gaze intense. Then he gave her a nod and turned his attention to her ankle. When he rolled up the leg of her jeans, she saw how her left ankle swelled over her sneaker.

"There's a mess," he muttered. "The shoe stays on for now, but I'm going to wrap it for extra bracing." He pulled Ace wrap out of his pack and started to strap up her ankle.

She gritted her teeth at the wave of pain, digging her fingers into the sparse grass to keep from yelling. Or bawling. Logan's gaze flickered over her face, her hands, but he didn't stop.

When he finally secured the end of the elastic wrap, and the pain decreased to a tolerable throbbing, Rebecca pulled in a breath.

Logan squeezed her shoulder. "Brave girl," he murmured, before rising. "Thor okay?" he asked Jake.

"Paw's ripped up some, but it'll heal." Jake grinned at Rebecca. "Nice bandaging material, Red."

Logan glanced at the bloodstained chemise still wrapped around Thor's paw and snorted a laugh.

"Looks like we'd better go straight west till we cut the old Bear Trail and use the Cedar Tree crossing," Jake said.

Logan eyed the stream. "Agreed." He grasped Rebecca under her arms and hauled her up.

Pain stabbed through her ankle, but she managed to turn her scream into a hiss.

Logan's hands closed on her upper arms, steadying her. He pulled her arm over his shoulders. "You're going to use me and Jake as if we're crutches. If the going gets too rough or you can't manage, then I'll carry you."

Carry her? She looked at him in horror. She'd die before that happened. Besides, she wasn't the only injured one here. "I'll be fine. You should carry Thor."

Logan's eyes softened, and he brushed her cheek with his knuckles. "You're just a marshmallow inside, aren't you?" He glanced at the dog. "He has four legs; missing one will barely slow him down."

Jake took his place on her other side. Between the two of them, she felt like a midget, and he apparently caught her thought. "Okay, short stuff, grab on, and let's do this before it's too dark to see."

* * *

By the time they reached the lodge, Logan was drenched with sweat, and Becca white-faced with pain. No complaints from the city girl, though. Every time he asked if she hurt, she'd say, "*I'm fine.*" As a man, he appreciated her stoic bravery. As a Dom, he wanted the truth, but halfway down a mountain near sunset didn't seem the time for a lecture on honesty. Instead, he monitored her carefully, and when the tendons on her neck stood out, her lips tightened to a thin line, or her breathing turned shallow, he'd ignore her protests and have Jake put her up on his back.

The only other times she spoke on the trip down were to express concern for him and Jake. And the dog.

Thor, being Thor, led the way down, despite his hurt paw, and the white tip of his tail made a beacon in the darkness of the forest. Still in front at the end of the trail, he trotted onto the lodge porch and waited for someone to open the door.

"Probably wants supper now, the bastard," Jake grumbled.

Rebecca stopped just inside the door. "He needs to have his foot taken care of. I—"

Logan shook his head. *Marshmallow heart.* He and Jake had seen the trail in the mud of the streambed, the marks left by her hands and knees showing she'd crawled to Thor after she'd injured herself. He scooped her into his arms. "Jake can handle Thor."

He carried her upstairs, leaving Jake to reassure the swingers she was all right.

Despite her halfhearted protests, he stripped her of her clothing and put her into a steamy shower, joining her a second later. Seeing her there, feeling her naked body against him, eased the last remnants of worry inside him.

Fuck, but she'd scared the shit out of him.

Soaping up her body only deepened his anger. Vivid scratches stood out on the delicate skin of her arms. Another red line marred her cheek. She was so fragile and soft, and she could have died so easily.

When he tried to dry her off, she shook her head and pulled the towel out of his hands. "I can do it, Logan. My ankle's hurt, not anything else."

He almost growled at her then, but the fury inside him would have to wait for a more appropriate time. He yanked on jeans and a T-shirt. After tossing more pillows on the bed, he hunted up water and medicine, then prepared an ice bag.

For the comfort of his modest sub, he searched her suitcase for a nightgown and handed it into the bathroom. "Let me know when you're ready to come out."

A second later, she appeared in the door, her injured foot touching the floor slightly.

He carried her to the bed. Her fragrant body felt appallingly breakable in his arms, and he wanted to hold her. To take her. To beat her ass. He set her on the edge of the bed, handed her a couple of ibuprofens and a glass of water. "Take these, and I'll see how much damage you've done."

She swallowed the pain pills. "I think it's just sprained. It hurts less now."

"Uh-huh." Since he'd unwrapped the ankle in the shower, it had doubled in size. He palpated the bones carefully. He could see the way she bit back her groans. How her hands fisted in the covers. Fuck, he hated hurting her. A man protects his woman, and he'd done a lame-ass job. He should have told her more of the dangers, should have insisted she come with him to town. Should never have left her alone. He sighed and released her foot. "Without an x-ray, I can't say for sure, but looks like just a sprain. Lie back."

He strapped her ankle tightly enough to keep some of the swelling down but not cut off circulation, then elevated her leg on a couple of pillows.

She studied his handiwork. "You're pretty good at that. It looks almost pretty."

"Sports, military, wilderness training. I've had a lot of practice." He picked up the pillowcase that he'd filled with plastic bags of ice and draped it over and around her ankle.

A staccato rap sounded on the door, and without waiting for a response, Jake strolled in.

Logan scowled. "You ever consider I might be busy?"

"Later, I'm sure, but you won't jump her ass when she's hurting." The glint in Jake's eyes showed he knew what Logan planned to do to that pretty ass. "Here's some soup. It'll probably go down better than anything else right now."

He handed Rebecca a steaming mug and a plate of toast. Buttered, even.

One of the most popular Doms in the area, Jake could be hard as nails, but for a hurt female, he turned as soft as the butter on that toast.

"Thank you, Jake," Rebecca said, taking a sip of the soup and giving a sigh of enjoyment.

"My pleasure." He nodded at Logan and left, his boots thudding loudly on the stairs.

Logan turned and looked at Becca. Foot up and iced, water on the nightstand, food in hand. Pink colored her cheeks again, and the lines of pain had eased around her mouth and eyes. As his fear for her died, the urge to yell at her grew. He needed to leave and let her rest. For a bit. "Foot feel better?" he asked, just to check.

She wiggled her ankle slightly. "Just some throbbing now. I'm sure it'll be fine in the morning."

"You'll stay off your feet for a couple of days. And we'll get it x-rayed tomorrow if it still hurts at all." He could take her down the mountain in the morning, have it checked out. "Finish your food and take a nap. One of us will be downstairs, so if you need something, you yell. Don't get up."

She nodded, apparently willing to obey his orders.

That would be a change.

* * *

As Logan left the room, Rebecca felt tears prickle at her eyes. It had taken all her resolve not to break down and drench the man in tears again. He'd rescued her. And then he'd actually carried her every time she started to give out. Carried her. And taken care of her like she was his…his girlfriend or something. Surely he wouldn't have climbed into the shower with any of the other guests.

She sighed, knowing her emotions were messed up from exhaustion and fear. Her body felt like she'd run a marathon, so she did what Logan had ordered. Finished the food, drank the water, and took a nap.

Tapping at the open door wakened her. "Yes?" She blinked and looked around. Logan must have been in earlier, since all the bedroom lights were off. She glanced at the glowing clock. Ten thirty. She'd been asleep almost three hours. "Come in," she called.

She could hear footsteps, and then Matt appeared in the doorway. "Hey, babe. How are you doing?"

"Better." She grimaced. "I wrenched my ankle good, though."

"So I hear." He ran his hands through his hair. "I didn't realize you'd gone off by yourself. Why didn't you come and get me?"

"I didn't think I had time to run around looking for a hiking partner. I was too worried about Thor." And rightly so. He had been hurt and needed her. "Did you see him? Is he all right?"

"Yeah, Logan doctored his foot and wrapped up his paw." Matt grinned. "Thor had the gauze off in minutes."

Rebecca laughed, and the worry knot in her stomach loosened. Thor would be all right.

"Anyway, I wanted to ask you about tomorrow. I'd planned to leave right at dawn. Is that still going to work for you?"

Leave? The unexpected reminder hit her like a kick in the stomach, stealing her breath. They were leaving tomorrow. *I'm not ready.* She wanted to grab on to the bed and yell, *I won't go.*

Unrealistic, Rebecca. True, she'd never felt like this about any man before, but her home was in San Francisco. Unhappiness settled inside her chest as she realized that Logan had never said anything about her staying or even about seeing her again.

Maybe he felt shy?

Logan? Get real. Maybe she could bring the subject up? Somehow?

But Matt needed an answer now. Make plans now, they could always be changed later. "Dawn is fine. I'll meet you on the front porch." She nodded at her suitcase. "Can you leave me some clothes for tomorrow, and take the suitcase now? With my ankle screwed up, I'm not sure I can haul it down the stairs."

"Sure." He knelt by the suitcase and pulled out a bra and panties first, added jeans, and held up a top. "Will this shirt be okay?"

A painful pang shot through her. No more of Logan's flannel shirts. "Sure." She didn't even bother to see which one. "Works fine."

"Good." He set the clothing in a stack on the dresser, then picked the suitcase up. "I'd better go, so you can get some sleep."

She dredged up a smile. "See you in the morning."

* * *

After Logan returned from making the rounds of the lodge, he checked the main room. With Thor at his feet, Jake sat by the fire, talking with Ted and Vince. The two were managers of a recreational sports company, and his brother had wanted to get a good deal on new equipment for the lodge.

Logan nodded at Ted and Vince, then asked Jake, "Everything all right with the crew?"

"They're good. Most of them are in the game room; three headed for a cabin."

Logan had heard the bed creaking in cabin three.

"Want a beer, bro?" Jake asked.

A beer would go down good, but no. Logan's jaw tightened. "I have things to do that require a clear head."

"Ah." Jake gave him an understanding nod. "Don't be too hard on her. She meant well."

"She almost got herself killed." Bad enough that she'd be leaving to go back to the city. The thought of finding her body...all the stubbornness, the humor, the warmth gone, her eyes blank. He knew just what traumatic death looked like. His gut twisted, and he turned on his heel.

Once upstairs, Logan walked into the bedroom to find Rebecca reading a book that would have had to come from the bookshelf across the room. She'd been up on that ankle. Trying not to growl, he leaned against the door frame.

So pretty. Her hair waved over her shoulders in the colors of the sunset. Her flannel nightgown reminded him of the ones his mother wore, yet the outline of her full breasts under the soft material made his cock harden. He shoved his lust to the background of his mind.

First things first.

The master in him was furious that she had disobeyed him, disregarded safety rules, and endangered herself. Over the past few days, he had been a Dom to her, and he would continue to teach her, even though the relationship would end soon. *Temporary.* The word tasted bitter in his mouth. He shoved the feeling of loss to one side.

So far, she had learned the easy, fun stuff and had received a taste of light discipline. Would she still submit when he took it a step further? "Becca."

She started; then her sweet lips curved up, her eyes lighting in a way that made his heart melt. "Logan. Did you get a chance to eat and rest?"

"Enough." He'd grabbed some food but had been too pissed off to rest. "How's your ankle?"

"It's much better. No pain unless I try to walk on it, and even then, I can put some weight on it."

"Didn't I tell you to stay in bed? To yell if you needed something?" He walked over to the bed and stared down at her.

Chapter Fifteen

The growl in Logan's voice sounded more menacing than Thor's best effort. Rebecca set the book on the nightstand, then gave him a wary look. "I wanted to—"

"Now there's the problem, Becca," Logan interrupted. He sat beside her hip, the mattress compressing under his weight. His eyes, more gray than blue in color, sent unease trickling down her spine. "If I give an order, I expect it to be obeyed."

Her eyes narrowed. "If this is that domination stuff, you said it applied only in the bedroom."

He tilted his head, his eyes never leaving her face. "True. In a way. I'm a dominant, Becca, and my nature doesn't change. Outside the bedroom, you can disagree with me, and we'll work out a compromise." He took her hand, and the calluses on his fingers felt almost threatening as he rubbed his thumb across the back of her hand. "What happened today, more than once, is that you agreed to obey my orders, and then you disobeyed."

Disobeyed? "Logan, I'm not a child," she said, shocked when her voice came out hoarse. A shaking started deep inside her.

"No. You're very much a woman," he said with a faint smile. "And you're also a sub. My sub—for the moment—"

For the moment. Why did that phrase hurt so much?

He continued, "Which means I have certain obligations to you, ones that preclude letting you think you can get away with disobeying your Dom."

His firm words, the look in his eyes, increased the shaking until her fingers trembled in his grasp. She stared at her hand in horror. What was happening to her? She wasn't scared—not exactly—

"Becca, look at me."

She raised her eyes.

"We can handle this in two ways. If we are just friends and nothing more, I'll lecture you about safety and go back downstairs."

The thought hurt her chest and tightened her throat. "And the other?" she whispered.

"If I am your Dom for the rest of your time here, then you will be punished as a sub, and we will go on from there." His free hand stroked her cheek, the gentle touch making her feel as if she were being split in two parts. "A Dom/sub relationship, however short or long, exists only if there is trust and honesty between both parties. So this is your decision, little one. Your answer is either, 'Let's be friends,' or 'I submit, Sir.'"

His hand on her cheek warmed skin that had gone cold and kept her from turning away. His eyes penetrated her, gazed deep inside. She knew he could feel her tremble. *Think, Rebecca.* But her ability to think had disappeared along with her willpower. She couldn't tolerate the idea of being just friends. Not at this point. She swallowed, her throat dry. "I submit, Sir."

He nodded, no expression on his face. "So be it." He took her hands and held them firmly. "So I'm clear, this punishment is because you went hiking alone. You didn't even tell anyone where you were going." His voice roughened. "Another hour, and we wouldn't have found you. More rain is due tonight... You'd have died."

"Wh-what are you—"

"You do not have permission to speak."

Oh God, what had she done? Yet the feeling of his hands thrilled her, at least until he pulled her facedown across his legs. She ended up with her head and shoulders hanging down, her hips over his knees, and her feet still on the bed. Head spinning, she put her hands flat on the small rag rug and tried to raise herself. When he lifted her nightgown up and cold air brushed across her bottom, the awful understanding came swiftly.

"A spanking? No way." She tried to push herself back on the bed without success, then tried to drag herself forward off his lap. Her nightgown was caught on something— probably his fist—trapping her. A hand pressed down on her lower back. "Let me go!"

"This will hurt less if you relax," he said, as if she hadn't spoken, as if she weren't struggling to escape.

"You son of a—"

Slam! The blow hit right across her right buttock and stung like crazy.

"Ow!"

He paused. "Let me know when you feel sorry for what you did. Otherwise, I'll simply continue until my hand gets tired." A pause.

Slam. Slam.

"Damn you!"

Slam. A pause.

"I hate you, you bastard."

Slam. Slam.

"You're sick. Sadistic."

With each blow, his hand came down brutally, stinging worse than she could have imagined until her whole bottom burned.

"B-bast—" Her voice broke as a sob escaped, and tears spilled from her eyes. She hated him.

His hand stroked over her bottom gently. "You scared me, sweetheart. If we hadn't found you before dark…"

Slam. Slam.

She gritted her teeth, trying to keep the sobs back. Trying not to beg.

He continued as if they were having a conversation. "Even Thor wouldn't have been able to keep you warm enough, especially since you couldn't go searching for someplace dry." A pause.

Slam. Slam. Her fingernails curled into the rag rug.

"Jake and I were terrified, you know. We ran up that trail."

They'd run? She'd had a tough time walking up it. And then he'd carried her a good part of the way down. She'd been stupid. And careless. Her anger withered and died, and her resistance with it.

Slam.

"I-I'm sorry," she whispered. "Please... I'm sorry."

"There we go." He lifted her up and settled her on his lap. Pain streaked through her when her bottom rubbed on his jeans. She couldn't stop crying, the deep sobs hurting her chest. Confused and angry, sorry and hurting, she tried to push away from him. "Don't touch me," she choked.

His grip only tightened. His hand cradled her head, pressing her face into his shoulder. "All over, little rebel. It's done."

When he stroked her hair, she felt comforted and even more confused. He'd hit her and made her cry and now held her. "I'm sorry."

"I know, sugar." He kissed the top of her head. "But damn, you scared me." His arms tightened until she almost couldn't breathe. "I was so angry, I didn't trust myself to do this earlier. You wouldn't have been able to sit down for a week."

His words turned her attention to her bottom. "I may not anyway, you..." She sucked in a breath. "Sir."

"Nice save, little one." He picked her up in his arms and carried her into the bathroom, setting her on the closed toilet seat. She hissed as fire streaked across her tender butt. "Wash your face and get ready for bed. *Call* me"—he gave her a harsh look—"when you're ready to come back."

"Yes, Sir."

After he carried her back to bed, he walked around lighting candles. She watched, her emotions still churning inside.

He stripped, and she had to close her eyes against the sight of his naked body. He was so, so gorgeous.

She heard the crinkle of a condom wrapper and knew he planned to make love. Her mouth tightened. After spanking her. God, just the word sounded childish. He'd hit her and now thought she'd want to…to fuck? *Not happening.* Pulling the covers up to her chin, she crossed her arms over her chest, trying to ignore the way her nipples had bunched into points. When she felt the bed sink under his weight, she opened her eyes.

He lay beside her, propping his head up on one hand.

She scowled at him. "I don't want to do anything but sleep. *Sir.* I have a headache."

His eyes narrowed as he studied her face, and his jaw slowly turned to stone. "No, you don't." He lifted her chin and gave her a look that seared all the way to her toes and made her stomach quiver. "Lying gets punished, little sub, but I believe your ass is a bit tender right now."

His knuckles rubbed gently against her nipples, undoubtedly feeling the taut peaks, and his smile was pitiless. "I thought to be gentle right now, but you lost that privilege. Instead, I'm going to take you for my own pleasure, and I'm going to take you hard."

Her mouth dropped open, but before she could speak, he'd ripped the covers out of her grasp and rolled her on her stomach. Ruthless hands shoved her legs apart, never bumping or touching her sore ankle. He yanked her up onto her knees, putting her butt in the air.

She felt a second of coolness when he shoved her nightgown up. A finger touched her pussy, swirled through her folds despite her squirming. He gave a satisfied grunt. "You're wet, sweetheart. Very wet."

Something pushed against her pussy, and then he sheathed himself in her so forcefully, she cried out. Her hands fisted on the sheets as her insides quaked around him in shock. His knees shoved her legs outward, opening her even farther, and he seated himself so deep, he brushed against her womb. She was still in shock from his entry when he started to move.

No gentle, sweet seduction, this. His hands gripped her hips, taking all the control for himself as he hammered into her so hard, tiny grunts broke from her. And yet, in spite of the ruthless way he took her, her insides heated. Her folds swelled and throbbed as her need rose. She buried her face in the pillow, turning just enough to get air, realizing that was all she could do. Overpowered, anchored in place, she couldn't even push back. Couldn't do anything except take it.

The thought made the burning worse. She could feel herself tighten around him as shivers spiraled through her body. Her legs began to tremble. She bit her lips trying to muffle a whimper.

He gave a short laugh. And suddenly he slid a hand down under her body, stroking through her folds, stroking her clit with a firm, callused finger, the roughness against her sensitive tissues incredibly exciting. Her hips jerked, tried to move, but he leaned forward, pressing his chest against her back, bracing himself over her with one arm on the bed, the other between her legs, stroking, stroking...

His heavy balls slapped against her pussy, sending shocks through her. The rhythmic thrusting set up a pulsing inside her, each one increasing the seething tension. Her hands scratched at the sheets as she panted.

He pulled back, almost all the way out, and she whimpered. The return thrust through her swollen tissues brought a cry. Remaining deep inside her, he rubbed her clit, bringing her to the brink, then lifted his fingers and pulled his cock out again. Hard back inside, fingers again. Over and over, until she couldn't think of anything except the feeling of his fingers, of his cock entering her. She tightened further, her legs turned rigid, and her hands fisted.

Suddenly he trapped her clit between his fingers, using a firm, pinching pressure as he hammered into her.

"Aaaaaah!" The fierce coil inside her exploded outward, sending pleasure crashing through her. Her hips bucked against his hand, but his fingers only tightened, gripping her as her pussy spasmed around his cock in unending shock waves.

He slowed, stopped, and waited until the spasms turned to ripples. His next powerful thrust sent a blinding surge through her as her insides convulsed around the intrusion in another spiraling climax. Another.

Then he opened his fingers.

She screamed as blood shot back into her clit. When he slammed his cock into her, and another violent release burst through her, the top of her skull felt as if it blew off.

"Oh God. Oh God. Oh God." She buried her head in the pillow. Everything seemed too sensitive, and she tried to pull away. Her legs were shaking too hard to hold her up.

He laughed. His unyielding hands yanked her hips up, and the hammering started again, short and fast; his hands controlled her every movement. He angled her to where he wanted her, then gave a deep growl, and she could feel his thick cock jerk hard inside her.

He didn't move for a minute, just held her against him with an iron arm across her stomach. His breathing slowed, and then he tipped them both over, keeping them spooned together.

"Still have a headache?" he asked in her ear, his voice rough.

"You're a jerk."

He chuckled. "This is true." His hand flattened across her stomach, keeping her pinned against his hot body.

Eventually, he got up. When he returned, he had more ice for her ankle. He rolled her onto her back despite her sleepy protests. "Ankle up, little rebel," he said, kissing her cheek. "The swelling looks better."

He took her two more times that night, awaking her from sleep once with his mouth on her breast. The next time, he had his mouth on her clit, having slid so subtly into her dreams that she awoke orgasming. When she tried to move that time, she discovered he'd cuffed her wrists to the headboard and her legs—at the knees—to the sides of the frame. Still gasping, she struggled to get loose, only to have his mouth descend on her again. Light and teasing, forceful and fast. She lay splayed open, available to anything he chose to do, and he did it all. She came, over and over. When he finally relented, he moved up to suck on her nipples until they poked up bright red, then thrust into her, thick and hard, bringing them both to a shuddering climax.

After cleaning up, he put her ankle back up on the pillows and ice, then pulled her against his side.

"You're worse than a mother," she grumbled. "I hate lying on my back."

He chuckled and didn't answer. The jerk. And yet how he...*dominated* their relationship, turned her on in a way she still couldn't believe.

He stroked her breasts, fondling them gently. He liked to touch, she realized. In bed, he kept his arms around her or a hand on her like now. The way he played with her breasts, or just touched her, or ran his hands over her body, made her feel so...so beautiful. Desirable.

She rolled her eyes. Of course, being taken a ka-zillion times in one night pretty much had the same effect. She wrapped her fingers around his hand, feeling a quiver inside at the difference between his and hers. Darkly tanned, callused, muscular. His wrists were the size of her hands. He let her explore, propping his head up to watch her in the dying candlelight. After a minute, she kissed his palm and curled the fingers down.

When she released him, he stroked her cheek, a faint smile on his face. "You worry me, little sub," he murmured. "Did your parents forget to provide you with a talk button?"

She frowned at him. "What does that mean?"

"I expected a string of curses after your punishment. Instead you buried everything. Time to talk." His blue eyes were intent on hers. "How did you feel about getting spanked?"

She jerked her face away, only to have him grasp her chin and force her to look at him. "No talk button, sorry," she said, knowing already that stalling was hopeless. "It's time to get some sleep, don't you think?"

His thumb grazed her lips. "Did your parents spank you?"

Stubborn jerk. "Mom did once or twice." She tried to remember. "For running away once. For playing with matches."

"That's normal enough. Your father didn't spank you?"

She shook her head. "He moved out before I turned eight." Because she and her mother were fat and boring. Without thinking, she pushed Logan's hand away from her face.

His eyes narrowed. "Did he hurt you physically?"

"I said no, didn't I?" She edged her hips sideways to turn more away from him.

With a grunt of exasperation, he used one heavy hand to flatten her on her back. "It was verbal, then. What did he say?"

"Listen, Logan," she snapped. "I want to sleep, not play psychobabble games, okay?"

"Skinny," he murmured. "I remember. Your daddy preferred skinny."

She gasped, his words sliding like a knife into her heart.

"Uh-huh." He wrapped an arm over her, sliding her more tightly against his warm body. His hand squeezed her hip gently. "Becca, your father was a blind asshole. I like you just like this." He chuckled. "And I really like spanking curvy bottoms."

The pain still lingered, but she relaxed slightly into his warmth. "Why did you ask me about spanking? Did you think I'd be pleased?"

"Sometimes physical or even mental punishment can revive old problems. You reacted like a pissed-off woman. I didn't see anything deeper, aside from you getting turned on." His grin flashed. "But I might miss something important. And you need to learn to talk about your reactions, pet."

He'd watched her that closely? Then again, why should she be surprised? He always did. She pursed her lips as something he said registered. "I wasn't turned on."

"Oh, yes you were, or I wouldn't have been able to take you from behind without a whole lot more work."

When his eyes crinkled, she could feel the heat in her face. God, turned on by a spanking? "That doesn't seem right."

"People are all different." He grinned. "I enjoyed putting you over my knees and walloping your soft ass. Watching it turn pink and feeling you squirm." His hand brushed over her breasts, making her aware of how her nipples had peaked. "I could have chosen a different punishment, but I wanted to know how you react to pain within a sexual context."

She glared at him. "Pain is pain."

He pinched her nipple, and she felt the sting shoot straight to her core.

His eyes glinted with amusement. "Not exactly."

Her face had flushed pink, her eyes dilating. What he wouldn't give to teach her more about pain and pleasure. And he wanted to delve deeper into those problems with her self-image, apparently originating from her asshole father. But he had no right to take this further.

In fact, considering his exhaustion, he should leave right now before he fell asleep. "I'm going to check something downstairs."

Her hand slipped from his waist down his front, then wrapped around his rapidly reviving cock.

Talking about spanking her had definitely been a mistake.

Her soft pink lips curved in a smile. "Permission to assault, Sir?" she asked in a throaty voice. In a smooth move, she pushed him onto his back and wiggled on top of him, keeping her ankle raised. Opening her legs to straddle him, she slid down until her soft pussy pressed against his cockhead.

Well. He could always sneak away later. "Granted. Assault away."

Chapter Sixteen

Rebecca awoke snuggled up against Logan's side with his arm wrapped around her. The time on the bedside clock glowed red in the dark room. Five in the morning. Not long until dawn. Not long until she needed to get into Matt's car and leave this place. And Logan.

God, she didn't want to leave. Not like this, with no plans to see him again.

Why did she feel this way? She certainly wasn't in love with him. No way. Not after knowing him less than a week.

Besides he would fail her perfect man list within the first few requirements.

Number one: smart. Well, okay, he passed that one.

Number two: liked the city. She wrinkled her nose. Maybe she shouldn't count that, considering her second thoughts about the city.

Then she probably needed to also drop the professional requirement. Besides, a business owner, whether deep in the wilderness or not, was a professional.

But the feminist requirement, the not macho? *Fail and fail.*

What did it say about her, though, that his strength gave her thrills? That she wanted him to tie her to a bed and do things to her? Heat slid through her veins, pooling in her lower half as if to illustrate the point. *Sheesh.*

Come to think of it, he hadn't been a macho pig when they worked together on the trail. He obviously enjoyed arguing with her and conceded easily when she had a better idea. And in the games they played that afternoon, he hadn't acted as if she didn't have a brain. *Dominant in the bedroom; the rest was negotiable.* All right.

She scowled. He certainly didn't dress well, and he probably didn't like Chinese either. As if either really mattered, dammit. So why wasn't this overbearing, macho man asking her to stick around or to visit, or making plans to come and see her? He sure acted as if he liked her.

She bit her lip as butterflies made loop-de-loops from her stomach up into her throat. If he wouldn't say something, she would.

Hands lock around his arms. A knife slices across his chest, fiery pain following. His blood splatters the dust-covered clothing of his attacker. Pushing the pain from his head, he wrenches free of the man behind him. Making a fist, he swings—

"Shhh, it's just a nightmare."

Logan froze. He didn't move as the stench of sweat and blood and gunpowder drifted away, as screams faded from his hearing. Eventually he could hear the quiet breathing of someone next to him and his own rasping breaths. His hand wasn't in a fist but grasped a curvy hip. "Becca?"

A low laugh. "I never thought anyone's nightmares could be worse than mine."

She had no idea.

Her hand stroked his chest, and she snuggled closer. "Logan. Sir. I was thinking. We're good togeth—Uh, I really like you, and maybe... I'm leaving, but I'd like...I'd like to see you again. Maybe come back here or—"

"No." The word ripped out of him, born from the bloody haze still streaking his vision. He hadn't hurt her this time. What of the next? He sat up, dislodging her. "Becca..." He scrubbed his face with his hands—brutal hands that could kill, maim, shatter. "Our time together. I enjoyed it. But it's over."

The cutoff breath was all he could detect of her distress, and he didn't want to see or hear more. Thank God for darkness. He had too much pain welling up inside him to take on hers as well. "Go home, city girl. Go back to your life."

He rolled out of bed, not bothering to grab any clothing. He'd spend the rest of this god-awful night on Jake's couch and somehow manage to give her a gentler good-bye in the morning.

When the door closed behind him, Rebecca didn't move, just stared into the darkness. The candles had died while they slept.

Her side that had pressed against him slowly cooled. As his scent faded, a tear rolled down her cheek. She'd tried, dammit. She'd been a brave fucking woman and put herself on the line. And he'd shot her down cold.

Her stomach hurt, and her chest felt so squeezed by the pain that she could barely find air to cry. She wiped her face with her hands, not that it helped, considering more tears kept coming. She rolled over in the bed, buried her face in the pillow, and simply cried.

She didn't love him. No, of course she didn't. But he hadn't wanted her at all. Not even enough to speak politely. Obviously, she'd just been a convenient weekend...fuck. And after four days, he'd probably gotten bored.

She was boring. And fat.

Her stomach twisted, and she swallowed against the surge of nausea. Everything he'd said about liking her— liking her appearance—probably meant nothing. Actions counted. Did she see him here now?

Here? Oh God, get out of his bed.

Sobs hiccupped out of her as she dressed. She welcomed the pain in her ankle, something real and physical, able to overwhelm for at least a second at a time the ache in her chest. Grabbing her nightgown, she looked around the room. Nothing of hers left here.

As she stood there in the center of the room, she realized she'd hoped to hear footsteps, hoped that Logan would appear, that he'd tell her he'd been joking, or that he hadn't realized she cared that much. She roughly swiped her forearm over her eyes, and her lips tightened. *That he hadn't realized she was such a pitiful loser as to cry over a man who just wanted a weekend fuck.*

And yet her heart leaped when she did hear footsteps coming up the stairs. The door opened, and Matt's face appeared. When he saw her, he frowned. "You okay, babe?"

Her hands clenched, fingernails biting into her palms as she made herself smile. "I'm fine," she said lightly. "Just having a moment. My period must be due." Just because she'd kill any man using PMS as an insult didn't mean she wouldn't use it when she wanted to.

"Oh. Okay." Matt ran his hand through his hair and gave her a concerned smile. "Jake let me up here so I could help you down the stairs. Are you ready to go, or do you need a minute?"

Yes. There were reasons she had considered Matt perfect. And Logan really, really wasn't. She pulled in a breath, feeling her chest quake, and put weight on her ankle until the need to cry passed. *No more tears.* "I want to go home now."

* * *

Hours later, when the sunlight came in the window far enough to hit the couch, Logan woke. He took a fast shower, skipped shaving, and headed downstairs. Thor rested by the fire on a pile of blankets. Logan stopped to check him. The gash on his paw looked clean. "Idiot dog," he said, tugging on Thor's scruff.

He nodded at the three swingers lingering over breakfast in the dining room and walked into the kitchen. Somehow, he'd have to explain to Rebecca why there would be no visits. The thought of telling her—anyone—about his nightmares turned his stomach. Maybe she'd just accept a simple "weekend is over."

He spotted Jake at the sink, cleaning up burned eggs from a frying pan.

Logan eyed the blackened mess. "I take it Rebecca didn't cook?"

"Nope. She and Matt left at dawn."

A punch right to the solar plexus. Impossible to inhale. Yet he must have made a sound.

Jake turned, his brows drawn. "You didn't say good-bye last night?"

"I didn't know she planned to leave so early." She hadn't told him. Then again, why would she after he'd shut her down so cruelly last night? He'd never meant to leave such ugly words between them. Not that he could change the outcome, but he could have softened the explanation without being dishonest. He could have let her know how much he'd enjoyed her company. What a goat-fuck. "I never figured on sleeping this late."

Jake turned his attention back to the pan. "Not surprising, considering you haven't slept more than a couple of hours in days. Then you carried her for the better part of three miles. Knowing you, you also spent the night screwing. I'm surprised you didn't fall asleep on top of her instead of on my couch."

"I did. Next to her. That's why I moved to your couch." Logan scowled. "I don't usually have trouble staying awake, dammit." Since the night he'd nearly killed Jake, he'd *never* fallen asleep with anyone in the room.

"I know, bro." Jake rinsed the pan and set it into the drainer. "I think this was the first woman you've trusted since your divorce."

* * *

"You quit your job. You and your boyfriend broke your lease. And he isn't your boyfriend any longer." Rebecca's mother paced across the parlor, her stiletto heels clicking on the marble tile.

"That's a pretty fair summary." Rebecca selected a piece of celery from the china plate on the coffee table, then leaned back on the white love seat.

"You're too young to be going through menopause."

"No, Mother. I mean, yes, Mother. Too young. I'm just reevaluating what I want out of life." God, she hated celery. Waiting until her mother had walked in the other direction, Rebecca shoved the stalk into her purse for later disposal.

"Did Matthew break up with you?" Her mother turned, hands on bony hips, and frowned at her daughter. "Undoubtedly because of your weight. Just look at you, Rebecca. You need to go for surgery. After stomach banding, a plastic surgeon can—"

"Mother. I don't want surgery, thank you. And I broke up with Matt, not the reverse."

"But why?"

"I met someone"—the stab of pain never seemed to lessen—"and I realized Matt and I aren't all that compatible."

"Oh." Her mother pursed her lips. "Well. You'll have to bring this new man to dinner so Vincent and I can meet him. Perhaps this Friday?"

"I... We're not together anymore. Either." Four days, the shortest relationship in history. *Weekend fuck.*

"Honestly, Rebecca. You meet him; you lose him. And you don't think your weight has anything to do with it?" Her mother perched on the edge of a chair. "And why are you wearing that kind of blouse? Your breasts are so large that displaying them like that draws attention to them in a very unattractive way."

"Uh-huh." They called this a one-two punch, right? First Logan knocks her down, and then Mother grinds her into the dirt. But Mom had a point. Obviously she wasn't attractive enough to keep a guy.

* * *

Logan glanced over at his dog. Thor lay at the top of the porch steps, watching the road with big, dark eyes. The person he waited for never appeared. Logan understood. He kept hearing Becca's low laugh, seeing the glint of red hair, reaching for her soft body in the night.

"You two are making me depressed," Jake said, scowling at the dog, then Logan. "Go get the girl already. If you can talk her into working as a cook, I'll spring for her wages."

"No can do." Body aching from the work he'd done to keep from thinking, Logan leaned back in the Adirondack chair. "She's lucky to have escaped without any scars."

"What did she say about that?"

Logan frowned. "Nothing. I didn't tell her anything." *Oh, hey, I tend to kill people when I wake up badly*. Right.

Now Jake frowned. "Seems like that might be one of those...ah, shareable facts. Who knows? Maybe she'd be willing to risk it."

"I'm not," Logan snapped. Not willing to discuss it, not willing to risk it. His hands fisted every time he thought of what he might have done, especially since she'd actually awoken him from a nightmare. Twice, no less.

It was amazing that he hadn't hit her or tried to... Logan rose to his feet.

"What?" Jake tilted his head.

"She actually managed to wake me up from nightmares twice without me knocking her across the room."

"Did she now? Huh."

Logan rubbed his jaw. "How did she do that? You never could."

Jake thought for a moment. "Your nightmares might be mellowing, or you might trust her."

"Might be either.

"You know, you don't yell at night anymore," Jake said, tipping his head back against the chair. "Or sleepwalk either."

"No, thank God." Blood and death still reigned in his dreams, but at least he woke up in his own bed. He'd never thought much about it. "The nightmares themselves never seemed to improve," he said slowly, "but maybe they don't affect me as much."

"That'd be my guess."

But could he trust himself not to hurt her? He slammed the hope down. Just because she'd survived him twice didn't mean shit. He shook his head. "No, I don't—"

"Bro," Jake interrupted. "You didn't kill the little redhead, and she was in bed with you. Hell, I stood all the way across the room and you came after me."

Logan's eyes narrowed. Dammit, he wanted her, wanted her with him, in his bed, in his arms. But he needed to know he wouldn't hurt her. He eyed his brother. "You feeling brave, bro?"

* * *

After forcing himself to watch a war movie, something he normally avoided because they inevitably gave him nightmares, Logan had gone to bed.

Hot, dry air and sweat tricking down his back. The rattle of the gun truck bumping along the road, soldiers on each side, facing outward. Screaming. An insurgent runs at them and is cut down by two of the soldiers. Before the body hits the ground, it blows in a ghastly splatter of red and flesh and—

A loud slam. "Die!"

Logan jerked upright.

Grinning like a jackass, his brother casually leaned against the door frame. The door still shuddered against the wall.

Logan rubbed his face, feeling the sweat. "*Die?*"

"Seemed like a good word to set you off." Jake scratched his back on the wood. "Didn't work, though. Night, bro."

"Night." Logan dropped back onto the bed, adrenaline coursing through his veins like he'd chugged at least five cups of coffee. "Thanks." *I think.*

Chapter Seventeen

The weeks since Rebecca had returned to San Francisco had been busy. She should have been too busy to think about mountains or vacations…or men who didn't want her. And still at far-too-frequent intervals, a feeling would sweep through her as if she'd forgotten something or left something behind. She'd stop and check. Key in purse, purse on shoulder.

At first, she thought she missed her apartment, but she really didn't. Her job? But resigning had brought her nothing but relief. So she had to face the facts. She missed the mountain and the lodge so much that the memories were like a heavy ball in her stomach. When she cooked, she kept setting tidbits aside for Thor.

And when she thought of Logan—she tried really, really hard not to think of him—she wanted to go back to him so badly, she'd actually had her car keys in her hand a couple of times. At night, she'd roll over, seeking his warmth, needing his arms around her. How she could miss someone she'd known less than a week didn't make any sense. Yet everywhere she went, she listened for his deep voice.

She'd bought five flannel shirts her first week back in San Francisco.

Truly pathetic, Rebecca. With a sigh of exasperation, Rebecca walked out of her temporary bedroom and into Pepper's living room. She nodded at her tall, slender friend, glanced at the purple couch and shuddered, then dropped into a green cushiony chair. "I'm surprised your eyeballs don't bleed."

"Just because you look ghastly next to purple doesn't mean everyone does." Pepper grinned and fluffed her black hair. "Are you all unpacked?"

"All done."

"Jobless, apartment-less, stuff in storage. You've been busy." Pepper walked into the tiny apartment kitchen and reappeared with two beers. "So what's next on that itemized list of yours, my artistically anal friend?"

Rebecca swallowed some icy, dark beer. "It's mostly a list of what I don't want, so far. No more meaningless jobs. No more cities." No more boring sex.

"You sure you weren't doing drugs on that vacation you took?"

Rebecca laughed. "No. Actually I painted." And had lots and lots of sex. "That's what I plan to do now. I illustrated some children's books in college. I called up those contacts today and it looks like I can do that part-time." Leaving the rest of the time for painting. And there was a heady satisfaction in bringing a book to life. Even better, seeing a child enjoy it. *Is that a real fairy, Daddy?*

"Okay. Check mark on the work." Pepper tapped her gold-spangled fingernails on her beer with a clinking sound. "Where are you going to live?"

"Well, I can work anywhere as an illustrator." Rebecca leaned her head back. "But I'm not ready to make a decision on that yet." She could explore a new state. Go anywhere.

She pressed her lips together. Jake mentioned the men's periodic trips to San Francisco to pick up lodge supplies and have fun. When she'd handed in the key to her apartment, she realized she'd harbored an insane hope that Logan would show up on her doorstep. He'd smile and say she owed him a blowjob. He hadn't. And now she had no doorstep for him to find. *Damn you, Logan*. The ache in her throat made the next swallow of beer difficult. She forced it down.

But she did have that third item on her list to deal with. Before she headed out to some rural area where she knew no one, she needed to know if the spectacular sex with Logan was due to that Dom/sub thing or because of Logan himself. If she found another Dom, would he be just as good? She couldn't imagine it, but she couldn't ever have imagined she'd let someone tie her up, or strip her and put things...

"Whoa, girlfriend, you just turned red." Pepper grinned. "I think there's something you're not telling me. What exactly happened on that mountain? Besides you and Matt breaking up?"

Rebecca felt her face growing even hotter. Then she laughed. "Gorgeous man. Hot, kinky sex."

Pepper blinked. "You? Kinky sex?" She set her beer down on the coffee table and leaned forward. "Tell me, and spare no detail."

"No details, you voyeur, but I do need your help. And it's related to kinky sex." She eyed Pepper. Even with all the secrets they'd shared over the years, this might be embarrassing. "You pretty much know everybody in the city."

"Well, duh. I run a bar. Of course I know everyone."

"Um." Rebecca turned the bottle in her hands. "BDSM. You know anyone who's into it? I want to go to one of the clubs and thought a...guide would be nice."

"Holy mother. You are absolutely not telling me that you've gotten into bondage and—" Pepper's light blue eyes widened as she stared at Rebecca. "You did. You are." She fell back onto the sofa, laughing so violently, she choked, coughed, choked again.

Rebecca scowled. "You know, all this shock is pretty insulting. I'm not exactly a virgin."

"No but—" Grasping the back of the couch, Pepper pulled herself to a sitting position. "Okay, okay, let me think. Angela. Yeah, she'd get a kick out of showing you around. You met her. Lew's Christmas party, remember?"

"Tall blonde, spiked heels, and a skintight dress?"

"That's her. She's a Domme, so if you go with her, no one will hassle you. Unless you want them to."

Rebecca bit her lip and then nodded. No point in making a journey of discovery and stopping halfway. "Call her."

* * *

Not dawn yet. Logan opened his eyes a slit, keeping perfectly still. What had awakened him? No noise except the ever-present rumble of traffic in the fucking city.

A cool draft of air brushed across his cheek, although he'd closed the windows before retiring. And there was too much light.

Ah. The door to his hotel room stood ajar with the hallway light spilling around the edge. He heard the slight scrape of a shoe on carpet, coming from behind him.

Well, hell, he had a burglar in his room.

Adrenaline surged through his body as he forced his lungs to breathe long and slow. *Still asleep, see? Come closer...*

Another breath of a noise. Logan jackknifed off the bed, tossing the covers over the intruder's head. He came up behind him, grabbed, and—

"Fucking A." Jake's voice. Under the quilt.

"What the hell are you doing?" Logan smacked the top of his brother's head before yanking the blankets back off.

"You asshole," Jake growled. "Don't you ever sleep?"

"You've lost your touch, bro. I could hear you from the minute you started on the door," Logan lied. "What are you doing here?"

Jake dropped into the chair beside the small table. "Thought I'd give you one last chance to do a freak-out." He flicked a finger in a token salute. "You passed with flying colors, soldier."

"Dammit. I thought I'd get one good night's sleep, at least." Over the last few weeks, he'd been woken up every night. Jake had done the honors at first, and then every vet in the Yosemite area had shown up to help.

And here Jake had always said he wasn't into sadism. With a grunt of annoyance, Logan dropped down on the end of the bed. "You sticking around?"

"I rented a room down the hall, but I'm heading back in the morning. I wanted to make sure you were all right somewhere besides your own bed."

"Good point. Thanks."

"My pleasure. *Not.*" Jake rubbed his head and grimaced. "Why aren't you in bed with Red?"

Logan growled. "What kind of person disconnects their phone without leaving a forwarding number?"

"She did what?"

"Yeah. And her mail now goes to a PO box."

"She took a powder? Why?"

"Don't know." Logan prowled across the room, too revved to sit. "I'm damn well going to find out. When you get home, dig up the numbers for the rest of the swingers. One of them must know something, probably the asshole boyfriend."

"No problem." Jake glanced at his watch. "I should be there sometime early afternoon."

"Good enough." Logan dropped onto the end of the bed and looked at the clock. Two o' fucking clock in the morning. "And, Jake? The wake-up calls? Do this again, and I'll bust your face. And it won't be because of a fucking nightmare."

* * *

"Whoa." Rebecca walked into Dark Haven and stopped dead as a naked woman trotted past. Hard, nasty music came from the back of the nightclub. Couches and chairs scattered here and there formed tiny secluded areas. More tables and chairs sat off to one side near a long metal bar. People everywhere, the Goth look prevalent. A man walked by dressed only in tattoos and a loincloth. Lots of wrist cuffs, handcuffs, and ankle cuffs on both men and women. Some women wore getups like Angela's. Thigh-high latex boots with stiletto heels, skintight latex that pushed boobs up, metal arm vambraces. Not women you'd want to meet in a dark alley, no matter how short they were. One carried a whip clipped to her belt. Other women wore nothing but cuffs. Some went topless. There were bustiers and see-through clothing and miniskirts.

Angela laughed and slung an arm around Rebecca. "Welcome to the weird and wonderful."

"No kidding." Rebecca shook her head. "I feel like Alice in Fetishland." Thank God she'd asked for a guide. Otherwise this place could totally overwhelm her. She'd definitely received a wonderful guide. After arriving at Pepper's with a bunch of clothing for Rebecca to try on, the Domme had dispensed fashion advice and then moral support after hearing Rebecca's story.

Rebecca smoothed down the pleated vinyl skirt, wishing it were two or three inches longer. But at least the full skirt hid her hips fairly well, and the black corset pulled her stomach in nicely.

Angela ran a hand down her arm. "You look divine, and I still think it's a shame you don't walk on my side of the street. Now you're going to wander around. I'm going to stand off to one side so people don't think we're together. Otherwise no Dom will approach you."

Rebecca glanced at the bar. A couple of beers would go down really well right now.

Angela followed her gaze. "No alcohol for you. BDSM and impaired judgment do not go well together. Especially if you and your top don't know each other."

Two women brushed past, one a step behind wearing a big, buckled leather collar like Thor's. Huh. Rebecca frowned. An amazing number of people—submissives—wore collars, usually the ones accompanied by Doms. Studded leather, wide leather that kept the person's head held high, thin steel. Most had O-rings; some had chains that went to nipple clamps or wrist cuffs. Rebecca's eyes narrowed.

That night in Logan's rooms, Jake had said something... "*Gonna collar her, bro?*"

"Those collars," Rebecca said to Angela abruptly. "What do they mean?"

"It varies." Angela grinned at a woman chained to the wall. "Sometimes they're just plain useful." Then she nodded toward a gay couple. "But for people like Alan and Peter in a full-time, master-slave relationship, a collar is equivalent to a wedding ring. Or sometimes it can mean you're in a Dom/sub relationship, and you're not available. Meggie wears my collar when we come here."

Relationships. What had Logan said? "*I'm no full-time master.*"

"*It can just mean commitment. You know, going steady.*"

"*Enough, asshole*," Logan had growled. "*Not going to happen.*"

Rebecca fingered her neck, remembering how Logan would close his hand over her throat, never enough to cut off breathing, just enough to show his control. A collar would be a symbol of that. His control. And commitment. Why hadn't he—

"Honey, stop thinking about the past. You're here to have fun." Angela patted Rebecca's arm. "Remember, if it's not working for you or if you feel off, just say no. I'll be nearby."

Have fun. Learn something. *Keep moving forward.* "Thanks, Angela."

"Girl, you more than paid me. That picture you drew of Meggie kneeling in submission is the loveliest thing I've ever seen." Angela gave her a wicked grin. "Besides, I enjoy watching newbies in a club. Now go find yourself a Dom."

Rebecca sucked in a bracing breath and headed through the crowd, trying not to openly gawk at…everything. Well-lit stages on the right and left wall had crowds around them; one had two men demonstrating how to tie a naked woman in a ka-zillion ropes and suspend her from the ceiling. The stage on the right had an elderly man wielding a whip. The cracking sound and the red welts appearing on the young man bound to a post made Rebecca's stomach twist uneasily.

Angela said to go downstairs to meet people and actually use the equipment. Rebecca pressed a hand to her stomach to still the nervous feeling and blinked at the tight feel of the latex. After glancing over her shoulder to make sure she still had her escort, she walked down the stairs and paused on the bottom step.

Strange equipment was set up everywhere: X-shaped frames, cross-shaped frames, sawhorselike tables. Manacles dangled from a low beam. Long, waist-high, leather-covered tables had people tied down on them. A Dom dripped wax on the bare breasts of his sub. Rebecca flinched. The music from upstairs could barely be heard over the sounds of whips and other things striking flesh and the groans, moans, and screams.

Well, she didn't have to do anything she didn't want to do, right? She glanced around, trying to look available. "*Don't approach a Dom,*" Angela had advised. "*All the moves are theirs.*"

As she walked through the room, men came up to her. Doms. She'd talk with them for a bit, but when they asked if she wanted to play, she turned them down. A woman hit on her, then another man. After wandering back to the manacle area, she stopped to watch. What would it be like to be the one whose arms were restrained like that? The chained woman faced the wall, and another woman in a dark red leather catsuit wielded a long stick across her back and rump, starting lightly, but now Rebecca could see the skin turning red. Her stomach quailed until she realized the sub's throaty moans were obviously not from pain.

A man in his forties in a black suit stopped beside Rebecca, glanced at the women, then looked down at Rebecca. "Is this your first time here?"

"Um. Yes. I don't know very much about this." When she met his eyes, she got that sinking feeling almost like

Logan gave her, only without the God-I-want-you jolt. "Um."

He smiled and stepped slightly closer, invading her personal space. Deliberately. Dark brown eyes watched her, reminding her so much of Logan that her breath hitched.

When he frowned, she pushed Logan out of her mind. This Dom stood almost six feet with level, broad shoulders. Silver flecked his neatly trimmed black hair. His face appeared finely chiseled, almost aristocratic in comparison with Logan's rougher features. But he had the very same overwhelming sense of authority.

"Are you here with someone?" His voice was deep and smooth.

She shook her head.

"You look like you'd like to play." He made the statement and waited for her response.

"Um. Yes. A bit." *I think*. She bit her lip. He seemed nice and definitely experienced. Not strutting like the first Dom she'd met, and not pushing and touching right away like the second Dom. He had the confident air that Logan and Jake had, like you could toss him into any situation and he'd know what to do.

And he watched her the same way Logan had.

He held out his hand. "My name is Simon. I'm not new in the community if you'd like to ask around first. You need to be comfortable with whomever you choose. And start slow."

"I'm Rebecca." She shook his hand and then caught sight of Angela standing a few feet back, watching. The woman smiled and nodded approval.

Simon turned and caught the exchange. "Angela," he said. As the Domme walked over, Simon tilted his head, glancing between them. "Yours?"

"No. She's a friend who I'm babysitting as she tiptoes into the scene." She glanced at Rebecca. "He's experienced, highly regarded, and"—she grinned—"strict but fair."

Simon's lips curved. "Quite a reference."

Rebecca sucked in a breath. Decision time. He was handsome and definitely a Dom, but she didn't feel any sexual attraction at all. Still, she had to start somewhere. "I think I'd like to try."

Simon held out a hand almost as big as Logan's. She put her hand in his, feeling safe and scared at the same time, but still nothing sexual. That seemed strange.

To her surprise, he didn't take her toward the equipment but over to a nearby couch. He sat beside her, keeping her hand in his. "Have you done anything related to BDSM before?"

She flushed.

"I'll take that as a yes." He massaged her hand gently. "Tied up?"

She nodded and kept nodding as he ran through a list: breast clamps, spanking, and toys.

"Anal sex?"

The memory of the thing, the plug, that Logan had put into her made her shudder. "No. Not really."

He chuckled. "I see. Flogging, whipping?"

She edged away from him.

"It's not something I'd do with a new sub anyway. Not the first time." He squeezed her bare shoulder, his grip reassuring rather than sexual. "Submission? Orders? Positions?"

"Some."

"Excellent." He pointed to the floor. "Show me what you learned."

She slid off the couch onto her knees, putting her hands behind her back, too embarrassed to open her legs, even though she'd worn panties.

He lifted an eyebrow. "He must have been new to the scene to have taught you so poorly."

Her face flared with heat, but the idea of him thinking badly of Logan had her spreading her legs open as he'd taught. "I'm sorry, Sir," she whispered.

"Ah. Modesty rather than inadequate instruction." He studied her for a minute. Longer. She kept her eyes on her knees. "Look at me, Rebecca."

She looked up at him. He leaned forward and ran a finger over the top of her bustier, touching her, reminding her of—

He must have seen the flinch she couldn't conceal. His hand dropped. "Tell me about the Dom who taught you. How long were you with him?"

"Four days."

"Must have been a very intense four days." He leaned back on the couch, his eyes focused on her face. "When you were learning all this, were you also having sex?"

For a second, she wanted Logan so badly, she could have cried. "Yes," she whispered.

Simon's smile was faint. "You obviously care about him, Rebecca. Why are you here?"

She looked down. How could she tell a perfect stranger about her doubts? A hand under her chin tilted her head up. He caught her gaze with his. "Answer me."

"I wasn't sure if what I felt was because of the...the submission stuff or because of him. I thought I should know that."

He released her. "Amazing insight, pet. And what have you discovered?"

"I think it's him." The answer felt right and yet opened up all sorts of other problems.

"I think you're right. But you are submissive without a doubt, Rebecca. If it doesn't work out with your man, keep that in mind when you look for another." Simon leaned back, rested his arms on the back of the couch, and studied her. Sexual or not, she still felt vulnerable under his dark gaze. "BDSM doesn't have to be about sex, you know. Would you like to try some of the equipment without worrying about that?"

"Really?" She glanced at the manacles, realizing the women had left.

He gave a deep laugh and smoothly rose to his feet. "Come along, little one. I'll give you your next lesson."

Grasping her arms, he set her on her feet. "What is your safe word?"

A shiver ran through her as he led her forward, her wrist in his grasp. Not her hand. She wasn't an equal. "Red, Sir."

"Good choice."

When she started to face the wall, he turned her around. "I want to see your face, and you need to be able to see mine." His lips quirked. "It's a different feeling too, seeing who's out there."

He had commanded her attention so thoroughly, she hadn't realized people were watching. Her face heated, and she took a step away.

His face turned cold, and his voice chilled. "Rebecca."

She froze.

"If something becomes too much or you cannot tolerate this, use your safe word. Otherwise, you're getting restrained. Right now."

Oh God, oh God, oh God. But she held still and let him buckle the cuffs around her wrists. Her breathing sped up, but at least she could move her arms a bit. Even scratch her nose.

He studied her, then walked over to the wall and tightened the chains hanging from the beam. Now the leeway disappeared as the manacles pulled her arms tightly over her head.

The feeling of being restrained and vulnerable sent funny sinking sensations through her with each breath, like the floor she stood on wasn't quite solid. Her thudding heart seemed to have moved up into her throat.

"Look at me, Rebecca." Simon's body blocked her view of the people watching. His dark eyes were intense as she lifted her gaze to his. "That's a good girl." He cupped her cheek, his hand warm and comforting.

As she tugged on the chains, trying to get used to the quivery feeling inside, he asked, "Do you like being restrained?"

She wanted to glare at him. Just like Logan, asking impossible questions, trying to plumb emotional depths.

"Rebecca, when I ask a question, I expect an answer, not a glare."

His reprimand shuddered down through her bones, making the quiver in her stomach worse. "It's scary. I don't know. I..."

"Giving control up can be a need that's not necessarily comfortable, especially at first." He tilted his head. "And being restrained in public? Do you enjoy being watched?"

She tried to shrug but couldn't move even her shoulders, and that sent another of those weird feelings through her. "It doesn't seem to matter that much."

He put his fingers into her cleavage, right over the hooks of her bustier. "If I stripped this off, would you feel the same way?"

Naked? Instinctively she yanked on the restraints and got nowhere.

He laughed. "Obviously not. Modest little sub, aren't you?" Rebecca looked past him, out at the crowd. To have them see her without clothing, her big hips on display... Her gaze crossed another's, and her breath strangled in her throat.

Unwavering blue eyes in a tanned, cold face. Legs apart. A leather vest showing off the muscular arms crossed over his chest. *Logan.* Her heart started to pound so hard, the entire crowd must have heard it. Simon surely did, for he turned around to follow her gaze.

Without a word, he walked away, walked right up to Logan, leaving her hanging from the chains. She yanked on the cuffs, and the pit of her stomach twisted. He was here. The surge of pleasure dimmed under the onslaught of questions. What would he think, seeing her like this? Seeing her with Simon?

And then she remembered that Dark Haven was a popular BDSM club. He hadn't come here to see her. As her hope died, she sagged in the chains. She tried to look away from him, and even knowing the truth, she still couldn't.

Chapter Eighteen

"Look at her," Simon said. "She wants to yell for you so bad, she's almost choking with it."

Logan smothered the red fury that his little rebel had allowed someone else to touch her. "I hadn't expected to find her out trolling for company," he growled.

Simon slapped his back lightly. "Actually, she's trying to discover if her head-over-heels reaction to you is because she just likes the lifestyle. She wanted to see if she can be turned on by any Dom."

"You have got to be joking."

"True, old friend. And damned canny of her, I thought."

Logan's eyes narrowed. "You realize that if you managed to arouse her, I'm going to rip your guts out."

"Lucky for me that she wasn't interested, then," Simon said lightly.

Lucky for them both. He'd seen Simon take on a drunk twice his size, and within less than a minute, the guy landed on the ground with a fractured jaw and several busted ribs.

"Logan," Simon said seriously. "She's delightful, and I would have enjoyed taking her further into the scene. I'm not the only one either, but she wasn't interested in anyone who approached. She's with me only because I'm a strong Dom, and she wanted to make sure."

Logan nodded to the chain station and raised his eyebrows.

"I asked her if she wanted to try some of the equipment while she's here." Simon grinned. "You'll forgive me if I thoroughly enjoyed her reaction to being restrained in public for the first time."

The last of the rage ebbed out of Logan's veins. He drew in a controlling breath, then turned so he could see his sub and Simon at the same time. "For her sake, I'm glad she found you." He frowned at Simon, who looked like a fucking *GQ* model, dammit. "For my sake, I'd rather she'd chosen some pimple-ridden wimp rather than the most popular Dom in Dark Haven."

Simon grinned. "I still struck out. I'll bow out at this point before you break your hand on my face."

"I appreciate it." Logan began to relax and enjoy the sight of his little rebel. Her red hair frothed over pale, freckled shoulders. Her breasts almost spilled out of the tight corset, just begging to be touched. A short, full latex skirt bared her legs. Damn, she was gorgeous, and he'd turned harder than a rock seeing her in chains.

When his gaze returned to her face, he frowned. Her eyes were still focused on him, but the stunned joy had changed into uncertainty, even sadness. And grief? What the hell was going through her head?

Logan glanced around. Simon had taken a chair nearby, obviously planning to watch for a while. "Simon, what did you say to her just before she saw me? It elicited a nicely terrified reaction."

Simon let out a laugh. "She said being in front of a crowd didn't bother her that much. I asked her if she'd feel the same if I stripped her."

"Well, then, strip her I will." After he figured out why she was looking at him with those unhappy eyes.

"I'd better go talk with her watchdog and keep you from being ripped apart." He nodded toward a tall Domme, one of the club regulars, who watched them intently. "Your sub is a careful woman."

Logan tilted his head, received the same back from the Domme. "Thanks, Simon." He stood for a minute or two, just watching Rebecca. He wanted to hold her so badly that he had to force himself to walk slowly as he approached.

Her eyes fixed on him. "Logan?" she whispered, straining at the buckles around her wrist. "What are you doing here?"

"Seeing you, little rebel. And what are you doing here?"

To his surprise, her gaze turned down, her lips drooping. "I'm sorry. I didn't know you liked to come here. I'll leave."

Leave? She would leave because of him? Anger stirred inside him. This didn't sound like someone head over heels about him. But he'd seen the pleasure in her eyes upon seeing him, before her head had kicked in. So her brain told her...what? "Why would you leave now, Becca? I came here to find you."

Her head jerked up, again that joy, and then it faded again. "Sure you did. Just let me down, Logan."

"You don't think I might have changed my mind and come after you?"

"Right. Every guy wants a plump body in his bed." Her lips tightened. "Stop messing with my mind and unbuckle me."

Someone had done some messing with her mind, but it hadn't been him. Guilt washed through him then, as he realized his nasty slap-down hadn't done her self-image any good at all. He'd thrown her out of his life without giving her any reason, so mentally and emotionally she'd gone down the same wrong track she'd been following for years.

He needed to solve this problem before they could move on. He eyed her, arms nicely restrained. Feeling like she did, he wouldn't get her in this position again.

Looked like this was the time and this was the place.

And the beginning of the solution would have to start with him. The thought of talking about his nightmares and Jake twisted his gut. But he owed her this. He'd kept information from her, and she'd suffered for it.

Logan stood in front of her, watching her with unreadable eyes. Rebecca blinked back tears. Damned if she'd look all sniffly in front of him. "Let me down. Now."

"Do you remember me telling you that there must be honesty between a Dom and sub?"

He obviously wouldn't help her until he had his say. Too bad. She didn't want to listen. Not anymore. "Logan. I want down." She felt her lips tremble. *I want to go home.*

He moved forward, standing so close, his chest touched her breasts. His hand cupped her cheek. "Easy, little rebel."

At the affectionate term, her eyes filled, and she tried to pull her face out of his hand. If he acted nice to her, she'd cry.

This time he used both hands to hold her face so he could look into her eyes. "Becca. I absolutely did not make you leave because of how you look."

"Sure."

His grip tightened. His eyes closed, and he drew in a deep breath before pinning her with that gray gaze again. "I gave Jake that scar on his face."

Her mouth dropped open, and she looked at him in disbelief.

"I've had nightmares since my discharge. Years. I can't— couldn't tell where the nightmare ended and reality began. A few years ago, Jake woke me up, and I tried to kill him." He pressed his forehead against hers, and she could feel his breath on her face. "Since then, I've never *slept* with anyone. Until you. Our last night together, I had a nightmare. Fuck, sugar, when you woke me up, I thought at first I'd hurt you." He rubbed his cheek on hers like a big cat. "That's why I sent you away."

She'd never heard him use the *F* word before. He *had* been shaken when he woke from the nightmares. She remembered that. "Nightmares." His scent surrounded her, so familiar and wonderful that her heart skipped a beat.

"Uh-huh." He took an audible breath. "When I didn't hurt you, I figured something had changed over the years.

Jake helped me test my control. It looks like I can wake up without trying to murder anyone around me." His lips curved, although his eyes remained cold. "Do you understand why I sent you away?"

Well, she knew he had nightmares. But that he really wanted her? "I've seen your nightmares," she said.

His gaze intensified. "A yes-no question usually gets a yes-no answer. Becca, do you believe I came to the club looking for you?"

He loved honesty so much; she'd just give him some. "No."

"Because you think no one likes lush women. Is that correct?"

She nodded.

"Got it." His hand fisted in her hair, and he tilted her head back to take her mouth. His kiss was hard, almost punishing, but oh God, she didn't care. His lips gentled, slid over hers. "Simon said you wanted to play. Is that correct?"

A tremor went through her. Playing with Logan was far, far different from with a stranger. But she wanted him so badly. One more time, even if she knew how it would end. She licked her lips. "Yes."

He nodded. His jaw tightened. "Then we'll play, sugar. What's your safe word?"

"Red."

"Good. Since you don't mind being on display"—his eyes gleamed as he studied her face—"you might as well do a good job." His fingers slid into her cleavage, and he began to pop open the hooks to her bustier. One by one until her breasts were completely exposed.

"Logan, stop," she hissed.

"What did you call me?" he asked, undoing the last few hooks.

"Loga—I mean, Sir."

He undid the last hook and tossed the corset off to one side. And then he actually cupped her breasts, right there in front of everyone.

She shook her head frantically, trying to ignore the thrill the feel of his hands sent through her.

He frowned at her. Not only did he keep his hands on her, but his thumbs circled her nipples in a way that made her pussy clench. "Is this my body to play with, sub?"

"But..."

He raised his eyebrows in query.

"You said you didn't share," she whispered. She could feel the way her nipples tightened.

"No one may touch," he murmured. "I don't mind if they watch." And he bent over and pulled a nipple into his mouth, sucking so powerfully, her back arched and pleasure sizzled straight to her pussy.

When she yanked on the chains, nothing moved.

"You can't get away, little sub. I can take my pleasure in any way I want, and you can't do a thing to stop me." He pinched her breast lightly, his lips curving at her gasp. His hand slipped under her skirt, and he frowned. "No underwear in the club. My rule. Am I clear?" His steely eyes trapped hers as he waited for her reply.

She nodded.

He ripped open one seam, then the other, and her panties dropped to the floor. Her skirt followed. She barely had time to feel the cool air before his fingers touched her pussy, stroking through her folds. *Sliding.* "You're wet, little rebel," he said in a deep voice, his eyes on her face. "For someone who doesn't like being shown off in public, you're awfully aroused."

She closed her eyes in shame, then jerked when he thrust a finger into her. His thumb circled her clit until she could feel it tightening. Burning. Urgent need seared through her.

He stepped back, leaving her hanging there. "You're naked, Becca. Everyone can see every inch of you. All those flaws you try to hide."

His words hit her like blows, and she gasped, tried to cringe, only the chains held her up. She couldn't hide, couldn't flee. She closed her eyes.

Merciless fingers grasped her chin. "Look at me."

She met his eyes, trying not to shame herself further by crying.

"I like my women soft and round." His blue gaze burned into hers. "I don't lie, Becca. I love your body, every single curve, every dimple, every scar."

She shook her head, unable to believe him.

"Sugar, I'm not the only one who prefers curves." He glanced behind him, and she realized there were an awful lot of people watching. Her mouth dropped open as humiliation streaked through her. "Considering we're not putting on much of a show, they're here because they like what they're looking at. That would be you." His hand fondled her breast, sending heat swirling through her.

"And you don't believe that either, do you?" He sighed when she shook her head. "Okay, then, I'll ask."

He turned around. "My little sub doesn't believe anyone likes soft, round women. Do any of you prefer bodies like hers?"

Applause and cheers made her eyes widen. *God, let me down. Let me hide.* Shivers ran through her.

"Good. Let me take it one step further, since she's vulnerable right now, and I want to drive this into her head. I think she's eminently fuckable. Would anyone who agrees take a step forward."

Chairs screeched as men—and a few women—rose to their feet, crowding forward. So many eyes, and yet they all showed the same thing. Desire. And pleasure at looking at her.

Her mouth dropped open.

"There we go. A dent in the disbelief." Logan moved forward, pulling her against him, and kissed her, taking her lips over and over, possessing her mouth, showing his enjoyment. He moved back and studied her for a second. God, she wanted to hold him so badly.

He nodded at her, and then he walked away, leaving her there. She bit back her first instinct, to cry out for him. He didn't go far, just to his black bag. He pulled out a whiplike thing. It had a long leather handle and a multitude of leather strands. "This is called a flogger."

She shook her head, trying to back away and getting nowhere.

"Becca, do you trust me?" He held her eyes. "Do you trust me enough to try something new? Do you trust me not to hurt you past what you can bear?"

She bit her lip. He wanted this. It seemed so wrong to agree, but she did trust him. She managed to nod despite how stiff her body had gone.

"Use your safe word if you need it, sugar."

Closing her eyes, she braced herself for pain. Something stroked down her leg, soft, almost tickling. Her eyes flew open.

Not speaking, he brushed her legs with the strands of the flogger, letting them trail down her skin. It had a sensuous feel like suede. The stroking moved over her breasts, her arms, her neck. Her skin grew more sensitive until she strained forward.

Then he stepped back and, with a smooth movement of his wrist, sent the strands over her leg. It felt like being hit with a bunch of tiny sticks. No sting, no pain. In a gentle rhythm, he sent the strands up and down her body until her insides seemed to vibrate with the flogger.

Then he stopped and moved forward, putting his hand between her legs, playing with her. This time, he rubbed her clit with that knowledgeable callused finger, one side, then the other, over and over, until she pushed out, trying to get more. She could feel herself coiling tighter and couldn't believe he could actually make her forget the people, yet it didn't seem to matter, not with his body so close, with his eyes capturing hers.

He stepped back before she could come, and she almost whimpered.

He started to hit her with the flogger again, more forceful than before, but the tiny thuds didn't hurt, not that much.

"I came to town only for one reason," he said. "To find you." The flogger struck her calf slightly harder. "Your phone had been disconnected." The other calf received a blow. His jaw tightened, his gaze flicked over her face, her hands, her mouth, her arms. Nothing broke into his concentration as the flogger hit in a complicated pattern, up and down. Each blow shocked a bit more, hurt a bit more, and her clit grew so tight, it felt as if someone was pinching it.

"Your apartment is rented out already," Logan growled. "Were you deliberately trying to lose me?"

Her insides were coiling tightly until that question shocked through her, and she shook her head. *No no no.*

He came forward again, cupping one breast in a callused hand and kissing her lips so possessively, her knees buckled and she sagged in the restraints. A finger into her pussy shot her back into arousal. He stepped back, and the flicking started again; this time the rhythm somehow coincided with the pulsing in her clit—or caused it—until she had to bite back a moan.

"I called Matt, and he gave me your friends' numbers." The whipping began to actually hurt, but somehow each pain turned to arousal, searing through her nerve pathways to her pussy. Each thudding blow brought her closer and closer to orgasm. "I went to see Pepper, and she sent me here."

He'd really looked for her. It hurt now, the flogging. The pain seemed to short-circuit her brain as her emotions surged up and down. *He wanted her. He said so.* But he couldn't possibly. Not really. She moaned.

"Simon seems to think you want a relationship with me." Logan's voice paused, but the flogger never stopped.

Her body hurt and somehow still seemed to be floating.

"Do you want to be with me, little rebel?"

Her mind had separated from her emotions, and only sensation remained, that and his words cutting into her, through all her defenses. "Yes," she whispered and moaned. "I want you." Everything kept coiling inside her tighter and tighter. The strands felt like stroking fingers on her body.

Suddenly Logan whipped across her breasts for the first time, the stroke lighter but shocking over sensitive nipples. The roaring came out of nowhere, a massive welling up of exquisite pleasure, throbbing from her core outward. Her back arched, her head tilted back. She could hear her own cries, and it didn't matter. All she could do was feel.

"You gave me the right answer, my little rebel." Logan's firm hands unbuckled her legs, then her arms, and a strong arm curled around her waist to hold her up. He pulled her into a tight embrace, tucking her head against his shoulder and rocking slightly back and forth, as if she were a baby. "Shhh, sweetie. You're all right."

Shudders ran through her continuously. Her face was wet. "Logan," she whispered. "Sir."

He pulled back enough to smile into her eyes, his hand gentle on her face. "And now I'm going to take you. You will have no doubt you're wanted." His brows drew together. "And who your Dom is."

Here? Wait...

He pulled her a few feet over to a hip-high bench and flattened her onto her stomach. She blinked, her head beginning to clear as he pushed her legs apart. One hand pressed against her clit, and an unrelenting hand pushed down on her lower back, holding her in place. Logan entered her with one hard thrust.

With a high cry, Rebecca came again, her back arching, her small hands gripping the edge of the bench. As her pussy convulsed around him, trying to milk him, Logan held on to his control. Barely. God, she felt good, hot and slick and tight. And he was going to take her here, in front of everyone, setting his stamp on her.

He'd never felt the need before, but he did now. "I want you too, Becca," he said, his voice rough with effort. "I want your body all soft and warm underneath me."

She was wide open, defenses down. Ready to hear and believe what he had to say. He moved inside her, slowly at first, to ensure he'd not erupt like a teenager, and then harder. Faster. "I want to hear you laugh in the morning"—

thrust—"to watch you paint"—*thrust*—"I want to show you my mountains"—*thrust*—"and dress you in flannel shirts."

Gripping her soft hips, he pressed deeper into her, feeling the after-climax ripples in her vagina and the tiny shudders coursing through her body. "I want to comfort you when you have nightmares and let you comfort me when I have mine."

He gritted his teeth, the pleasure so intense, his ears started to ring. Finally he couldn't wait any longer and hammered into her with a climax that started at his toenails, gripped his balls in a pitiless fist, and finally jerked out of his cock.

She lay limp under him, and from the intense rippling around him, he'd taken her with him. Only fair, since she'd taken a piece of him when she left.

He slid out of her, savoring the small whimper. After buttoning his leathers, he pulled her to her feet and then into his arms. Soft and round and lovely. *And his.*

Her head spun as if she'd been drinking all night, but she knew that Logan's arms held her up. His masculine scent of pine joined with leather and sex. His heart pounded hard under her ear, thudding in the same rhythm of the whip he'd used on her and in the same rhythm as the words he'd used. "*I want you.*"

His hand gripped the nape of her neck, and he gave her a kiss that had the world spinning again. Her pussy clenched as his other hand squeezed her bottom, stroking over her skin. His calluses felt like...

She blinked, realizing her bottom was bare. She was naked. She'd come, screaming, in front of a club full of people.

She jerked back from him in shock, saw the people watching, and hid her face against his shoulder. Oh God.

A laugh rumbled through his chest. "Back to being shy? A tad too late, Becca." His hand lifted her chin so she had to look at him. His eyes had gone back to steely, and his jaw tightened. "Now that your head is clear, perhaps you remember saying you wanted to be with me. Is that still true?"

Her stomach fluttered as she nodded.

His big hands closed on each side of her face. "Come back with me to the mountain, Becca. Be our cook and paint during the summers, and in the winters we'll go wherever you want to vacation." He took a breath, and his gaze grew more intense. "And be my sub."

Her hands tightened on his shoulders. She nodded again.

"All of it, little rebel?"

"All of it." She smiled as joy whipped across her body almost like a blow from a flogger. "Sir."

"Well, in that case"—Logan pulled something out of his pocket and put it around her neck—"I'm marking you so I don't have to worry about you straying off with some asshole Dom. It says you're committed—to *me*—and you will wear this anytime we go to a club." He turned far enough to shoot a cold look at a grinning Simon.

She heard a tiny *snick*. Putting her fingers to her neck, she felt the thin leather collar. And a tiny padlock.

He waited, holding up the key, giving her the chance to protest.

She took the key and tucked it into his leathers' pocket, then pulled him down for a kiss that made the room break out in cheers.

 # THE END

Cherise Sinclair

Now everyone thinks summer romances never go anywhere, right? Well...that's not always true.

I met my dearheart when vacationing in the Caribbean. Now I won't say it was love at first sight. Actually, since he was standing over me, enjoying the view down my swimsuit top, I might even have been a tad peeved—as well as attracted. But although our time together there was less than two days, and although we lived in opposite sides of the country, love can't be corralled by time or space.

We've now been married for many, many years. (And he still looks down my swimsuit tops.)

Nowadays, I live in the west with this obnoxious, beloved husband, two children, and various animals, including three cats who rule the household. I'm a gardener, and I love nurturing small plants until they're big and healthy and productive...and ripping defenseless weeds out by the roots when I'm angry. I enjoy thunderstorms, playing Scrabble and Risk, and being a soccer mom. My favorite way to spend an evening is curled up on a couch next to the master of my heart, watching the fire, reading, and...well...if you're reading this book, you obviously know what else happens in front of fires. :)

Cherise

Loose Id® Titles by Cherise Sinclair

Master of the Abyss
Master of the Mountain
The Dom's Dungeon
The Starlight Rite

The MASTERS OF THE SHADOWLANDS Series
Club Shadowlands
Dark Citadel
Breaking Free
Lean on Me

"Simon Says: Mine"
Part of the anthology *Doms of Dark Haven*
With Sierra Cartwright and Belinda McBride

The above titles are available in e-book format at www.loose-id.com

Masters of the Shadowlands
(contains the titles *Club Shadowlands* and *Dark Citadel)*
Breaking Free
Lean on Me
Master of the Mountain
The Dom's Dungeon
The above titles are available in print at your favorite bookstore

CPSIA information can be obtained at www.ICGtesting.com
Printed in the USA
LVOW051952070313

323223LV00001B/92/P